The Displaced

Book 2: The Roar of the Rex

M.J. Konkel

ISBN: 9781983166426

The Roar of the Rex

Book 2 of The Displaced

by M.J. Konkel

Author's Notes

This is the second book in *The Displaced* series.

While the location is more or less real (several details were purposely changed), all characters (apart those used for cultural context) and events are a product of the author's imagination and totally fictional.

A fair warning to those who are uncomfortable with **foul language**: some of the characters in this book use language natural to them. If you're uncomfortable with such language, you should consider refraining from reading further.

I hope you enjoy the book.

Books by M.J. Konkel available from Amazon Kindle as e-books or paperback:

The Displaced Series
      Book 1: No Road Out
      Book 2: Roar of the Rex
      Book 3: Between Time and Space
Dinosaur Country Series
      Book 1: No Mercy in Dinosaur Country
      Book 2: Predators and Prey
      Book 3: The Definition of a Monster
Dangerous First Step
Boots of Oppression

Chapter 1 - DeJuan

San Francisco International Airport. Early October, in the autumn of next year.

Maybe for the first time in his life. Maybe for the first time in his life. If his flight had been on time, everything would have been fine. Maybe not peachy since it was half past one in the morning. But he would have been on a flight, probably somewhere over Nevada by this time, on his way to his destination.

Instead, he leaned against a counter and listened as he was told his flight was delayed due to some technical problem with an instrument. DeJuan asked if it were the type that could cause them to crash or something less critical like the controls to the seat warmers. The lady behind the counter did not know the type of instrument involved—she wasn't given the info—but it definitely was not the seat warmers. The seats didn't have those. And people said DeJuan didn't get sarcasm; he shook his head. The woman said it would be several hours before they could get the replacement part. She had been told the installation would be easy, but they couldn't do anything about it until the part arrived.

He slogged over to a bench and placed his butt on the seat as he cursed under his breath. Not at the airline lady but at himself. If he had arrived a few minutes earlier, he would have been placed on a different flight along with all the others who had arrived early. By the time he had arrived, however, all seats were filled on the alternate flights until after eight in the morning or were with a connecting flight that wouldn't get him to Minneapolis any sooner. Simply waiting was the best option he still had left even if he didn't like it. He cursed again, but then he heard his mother's voice in his head telling him he had only himself to blame. Thinking of her made him sad for a moment. If only she were still alive.

He glanced around. There were fifteen or so other unlucky souls near the gate who would also have to wait until the morning. Poor lady at the counter. She must have had to explain the situation over and over.

"This sucks!" he quietly muttered to himself. Oh well, just as well make the best of it. His bench was in a corner, and he sat alone. He laid down flat on his side and stretched out his tall skinny frame on the vinyl seat with his dark-skinned hand between his shaven head and the backpack he used for a pillow. Intent on getting some shuteye before he would eventually be allowed to board. It was making the best of the situation, but it wasn't the best situation. A fitting cap for a long hard week.

It seemed like he had just fallen asleep when someone lightly tapped his shoulder. He struggled to lift the heavy lids over his eyes, and then he squinted against the bright light. One of the airport staff leaned over him and seemed ready to prod him again. He raised an arm to fend her off, and the lady straightened up.

"Sir, are you flying on flight 309 to Minneapolis?" The lady smiled. No one should be smiling this time of the night.

"Uh-huh." He rubbed his eyes, trying to get them to stay open.

"Good news! Your flight will be taking off shortly."

He yawned. "I thought something was broken in the cockpit."

"On the airlines, we call it a flight deck. Anyway, it turns out they were able to fly the part over from the San Jose airport, and it is being installed right now as we speak. I was told it's an easy swap for the malfunctioning part and would only take a few minutes. We're now boarding, and departure will be as soon as everyone is aboard and seated. Just make sure you have your boarding pass and ID ready. Have a nice flight, sir."

As she turned away, DeJuan thought she sounded way too perky for the time of the night, probably why she had the job. He knew he wouldn't survive in her job. He stretched, grabbed his bag, and rose to board along with the others.

Stepping onto the plane, three flight attendants, one a few inches taller than the other two, greeted him and the other passengers. While he waited for a couple in front of him to stow a pair of bags, he commented to the tall one that he had thought they wouldn't fly passengers if it wasn't a mostly full flight. She replied the plane had to be in Minneapolis anyway for a flight to Atlanta in the morning.

He realized, due to the small number of passengers, they were probably going to get fast attention from the attendants. Too bad he wasn't going to take advantage of it because all he wanted was to shut his eyes and doze. Once he was seated, he asked for a blanket, and a flight attendant handed him one with a smile. Then she quickly moved on to another passenger demanding her attention. He rolled it up to use as a pillow and wedged it into the space between his seat and the window. He leaned against it and immediately dozed off to the low rumble of the plane's engines, vaguely aware they were taxiing toward the runway.

"Sir! Sir!" Someone was trying to wake him.

"What?" he grumbled. It seemed he had just fallen asleep again. Why would anyone bother him so soon? He had been in the middle of a dream, a bad dream, but the details were rapidly fading. What was it about, anyway? It came back to him. "Man! Was in the middle of a dream. Being chased by a dinosaur."

"Wow! Quite the imagination you have there. But we won't be seeing any dinosaurs on this flight. Right now, I need you to put your seat forward into its fully upright position. We'll be landing shortly."

He glanced at his seat not remembering putting it back. He must have done it while he slept. His eyes were irritated. Dry. He blinked as he up-righted his seat and glanced at his watch. Nearly four hours had passed since takeoff, but it didn't seem like he had slept that long. He adjusted his watch as he remembered Minneapolis would be on central time. He suddenly noticed a chill had set on him, so he unrolled the small blue blanket wedged against the window and laid it across his lap with the airline's logo side up.

The captain's voice droned over a speaker, "We will be landing in just about ten minutes at Minneapolis–St. Paul International where the local time is now 5:44. They are experiencing some local storms, so the ride coming in could be a bit bumpy. Make sure you stay seated and keep your seat belt fastened until the light goes off. If you are connecting to another flight, you'll want to check in with an agent as soon as we arrive since we will be coming in almost two hours behind schedule. We hope the delay hasn't been too much of an inconvenience, and we thank you for flying Sierra Air."

DeJuan glanced down and compared the reported time to what was on his watch. He needed for it to be correct, needed the precision. He glanced through the window next to him. Lightning flashed harmlessly below as they descended into the clouds, and then they popped through them. Beads of rain appeared on the window and raced toward the rear of the plane, only to be replaced by fresh drops.

Suddenly all the lights from the Twin Cities became visible. He loved seeing city lights from the air. The orderly, yet complex and varied patterns was the proclamation of civilization, yelling out to the universe, "We are here, and we are alive." The plane continued its bumpy descent toward the runway.

DeJuan pressed his face closer to the window. Something outside caught his eye, and his eyes followed it out to the tip of the wing. A mysteriously faint green glow emanated from there that was not from any of the plane's normal running lights.

Then it was as if someone had thrown a switch. Everything below went dark. He peered as far forward and as far back as possible through his window. Then he was pushed back into his seat as the plane ascended.

"No, no!" he yelled. "It can't be happening again."

"What? What's going on?" a man asked from the seat opposite the aisle from him.

"What do you see out your side of the plane?" DeJuan's pitch was elevated.

"Nothing, it's too dark. I see a few headlights from cars, but that's about it. Looks like the whole area is in a power blackout."

"Wouldn't you think, even in a blackout, you'd see more than a few car headlights?" DeJuan asked.

The man frowned and turned back toward his window.

"And the airport should have emergency power if this is a blackout," DeJuan yelled. He turned back to his window. Nothing, except for the horizon showing a thin line of not black.

He felt light-headed. He was sure he knew what had just happened. Panic threatened to shut him down. He had to calm himself, concentrate on his breathing. *Slow it down, slow it down,* he told himself.

After more than a minute went by, he felt back in control of himself again. He could not afford to do that again. Maybe never again. He had to be in control, and he had to stay there.

He sat for several more minutes and thought about the green glow and the lack of lights below. The plane banked around again, circling the airport. Or where the airport was supposed to be. He released his seat belt and marched up the aisle, challenging since the plane banked every few seconds.

The tall attendant stood up and blocked his path forward as he reached the front. "Sir, you have to be seated."

"I must speak to the captain," DeJuan said.

"That is not allowed. The door to the flight deck is locked, and you must sit down. Federal regulations stipulate you are required to comply."

He glanced down at her name badge and locked his eyes there. "Look, Miss Freeda, take a peek out the freaking window. You have any idea what just happened? Know where we are? This isn't

Minneapolis anymore. I have to speak to the captain. Immediately."

She glanced at the nearest window but held her ground. She reached behind her and picked up a phone on the wall. "Captain, it's all dark everywhere outside, and there is a young man out here who says he needs to talk to you. He says it's about what just happened. Do you know what he's talking about?" She listened for a few seconds, then hung up and turned back to him. "You have to take a seat, sir."

DeJuan reached around her and banged on the door. "Dang it! Listen to me. I have to speak to the captain."

Freeda continued to stand tall in front of him. "You have to return to your seat, or I will report you, and you will be arrested."

"I don't think there's anybody here to do that anymore."

Another man came forward behind DeJuan. "Calm down and listen to her, young man. You're going to get yourself into trouble."

DeJuan turned toward the man. "Don't any of you get it?" He scanned around at other faces for any sign of recognition of the situation. "This is the Brown's Station thing all over again. You know what I'm talking about, don't you? This time it got us."

"Of course everybody knows about that. But they're just experiencing a power outage. Don't be panicking the rest of the passengers," Freeda said.

The door to the flight deck opened, and the captain's face appeared. "Everybody, please take a seat and get buckled." The captain glanced at DeJuan. "You too, sir."

"DeJuan Jazkins."

"Mr. Jazkins—"

"Actually, it's Dr. Jazkins."

The captain sighed. "Dr. Jazkins, we are already aware of the situation. Please, take a seat."

DeJuan backed into the nearest seat and hoped the captain really knew what they were up against.

The captain raised his voice. "Listen, everyone. I want everyone to be in the back half of the plane. We're going to have to make an emergency landing, and it will be rough."

The noise level rose and everyone seemed to be talking all at once. Outside, it had just started to get faintly light on the ground below. Someone from the back who had been looking out a window shouted, "Where are we? Nothing's out there. Where are we going to land? What are we going to do?"

The captain sent Freeda back to calm the man down.

"Why can't they turn the lights back on at the airport. For crying out loud, they have no emergency lights?" a man asked.

"There is no airport down there, you moron," replied the man next to him.

A woman pointed at DeJuan. "That man's right. This is Brown Station happening to us." She looked to the captain. He didn't deny it.

"What is that below us?" Someone asked.

"That's the huge mall they have up here," someone replied.

Someone else spoke up. "We can't stay up here forever. There's a highway and a few roads down there by the mall. Maybe we could land on one of 'em."

"We cannot land on a road," the captain said. "There're overhead signs and overpasses. Besides, those roads are way too short and are not designed to take the weight of this plane. We're going to look for a flat field nearby and touchdown if we can find one long and flat enough. If not, we're going to have to ditch into one of the nearby lakes or rivers within a short hike to the buildings down there. We'll circle above until it's lighter down there, and then we'll pick out a landing spot."

Everyone talked at once. Some shouted. The captain raised an arm until the noise diminished.

"Why can't we fly to another airport?" asked the woman in the seat behind DeJuan. Her apparent husband, seated next to her, had called her June.

"There are no other airports here," DeJuan replied. "Those buildings below may be the only buildings anywhere on this world."

"What do you mean? Where are we?" June asked. "How did you get us in this mess?" She demanded an answer from the pilot.

"OMG! I think there's a dinosaur down there," a young woman shouted. Most of the other passengers tried to peek out of the windows. It was still dark down on the ground, but twilight made it possible to see a little of what was below.

"Have you ever landed in a field or on water before?" DeJuan turned to the captain.

"I've done it many times on simulators," the captain replied.

"Simulators? That doesn't exactly fill me with confidence," DeJuan said.

"The need to land in situations like this doesn't happen all that often. The simulators are accurate. I got this. Please go to the back with everyone else and get buckled for your own safety." The captain turned to the attendants. "I want you three to sit with the passengers. Try to keep them calm and listening to my instructions. Have them ready to put on life vests if it turns out we need to ditch into water. You three up to it? Are you good?" After they all nodded, he opened the door to the flight deck and disappeared.

DeJuan wandered back to an empty seat near the wings and buckled as the plane circled yet again around the same spot. Some of the other passengers gawked out the windows in awe of the dinosaurs while others appeared shocked by the situation. Although the sun had risen for the plane, it was still only twilight down on the ground. It would soon be light down there too.

DeJuan peered around at the others and asked himself why he hadn't taken the morning flight? Better, why hadn't he gotten to the airport sooner.

A tall husky man squeezed up the aisle and leaned over the seat toward DeJuan. "I am Father O'Brien.

Some of us in the back are going to gather for a prayer before landing. Would you like to join us?"

DeJuan was surprised. He would have expected a priest to be in robes or maybe a black suit. Certainly not blue jeans and a t-shirt. Of course, that was what DeJuan also wore. "Sorry, Father, but I don't believe in prayer."

"That's all right, my son. We will include you in our prayers anyway." The priest pivoted and returned to the back of the plane.

Half an hour later, they still circled over the same spot. Everything below them now clearly visible.

"Okay everyone, the Mall of America and the building just to the north of it seem to be the only buildings down there, so that's where we're headed," the captain announced over the speakers. "We're going to set down on a lake that parallels the river below us. I believe it's the Minnesota River. The mall will be just a short hike northwest from there. Attendants, make sure everyone puts on a flotation device. Folks, I'm not going to lie to you. It's going to be rough, so make sure you brace yourselves as we come down. But we'll survive this. You will all walk off this plane. You have my word on that."

The attendants stood and moved to the back. They helped the passengers put on the flotation devices and then headed for their own seats. Furrows above Freeda's eyes as she glanced back one last time toward the rear of the plane.

The plane circled around one last time, and then DeJuan's stomach turned queasy as they descended.

As he peered out the window, the ground came up fast, and then the river appeared below them. A patch of trees flashed past under them. A lake suddenly appeared so close Dejuan was sure they must be skimming its surface.

He pushed hard against the seat in front of him as he braced for impact. He wished he could see what was in front of the plane instead of only the view out the side. DeJuan always liked to know where he was headed. If they crashed into something, he may never even know it.

At the last moment the front of the plane came up again as if the pilot had changed his mind. DeJuan glimpsed a huge dinosaur in the river off to his right, a *Brownstasaurus*. Identified down in the Brown's Station zone, it resembled something out of *The Flintstones*, especially because of the poor optical quality of his window.

His body was jerked forward several times as the rear of the plane skidded over the water and bled their momentum. The lake wasn't going by the window as fast; they were slowing.

Then his head slammed forward into the next seat, and at that moment, he was sure he was about to die.

Chapter 2 - Emilio

Level Two North, clear. *Airplane?*" Emilio spoke into his mic with a smooth high-pitched voice people found pleasant. Marching down the walkway dressed in his mall security uniform, he looked sharp, despite being a little on the pudgy side. He had inherited his father's Latin American boyish facial features, and he kept it free of facial hair and topped with a short-cropped haircut.

He told jokes and had a well-deserved reputation for being a bit of a prankster. Just two evenings prior, he had made sure he was the first to arrive. He then taped a sheet of paper on the copier that read:

> *This copier has now been upgraded to voice recognition. Please make sure you speak in a loud clear voice when giving commands. Also, the voice recognition software may have to learn your voice. You may find you need to repeat your command until it is accepted.*

At the end of the night, Bill had been making the required copies of the nightly reports. He kept repeating "copy" over and over and getting louder and louder. Then Robin came over and tried. Joel just shook his head as he came over and pressed the run button on the display. Emilio burst out laughing, while Bill whipped forward his hand and ripped the fake instruction sheet off the copier. Bill was mad at him at first but soon had to admit it was darn funny. Before leaving his shift, he helped Emilio set it up again before the morning shift arrived.

Emilio giggled as he snapped out of his reverie, thinking he needed to come up with a new prank. It might take a lot of monofilament and some planning though. His problem was his drone was too loud. He had to think on it.

Joel's response came over the radio. "Yes. Good one. Level 1 South is all clear. I'm thinking *The Princess Bride*?"

"Absolutamente!" Emilio said. "Just saw that one with my little girl a couple of nights ago. Forget which channel it was on. Your turn, Bill."

"Ah, *Police Academy*," Bill said.

"*Police Academy*? No way, Jose. Not a classic," Emilio said.

"Is too a classic!" Bill replied.

"Give me a line from the movie," Emilio demanded.

"Um …"

Emilio gave Bill a few seconds. "Joel, what's the ruling?"

"Give me a minute here. I'll come up with one," Bill said.

"Sorry, Bill. Doesn't matter. It's a funny movie but not quite a classic. My thumb is pointing down," Joel said.

"Wouldn't you watch it again? I know you would. That makes it a classic. Doesn't it?"

"Sorry, you know the rules. Two votes to one. It's not a classic," Emilio said.

"Fine!" Bill sighed. "Your turn, Emilio. Duds."

"Can you guess—"

"Hey guys, enough with the fun and games," Robin interrupted. If Emilio were asked, he would have said she was plain looking with long straight hair and a cute face. She wasn't fat; she just didn't have the curves he and lot of guys liked. Not that it really mattered to him since he was happily married.

"There a reason you just interrupted my nominee for worst movie featuring a dinosaur?" Emilio asked. Movies was the night's topic for Hall of Fame or Hall of Shame. They played a lot of radio games while on patrol since not much typically happened during the graveyard shift at the mall. Robin was in the security control center, surveying the video screens.

"Three vehicles just sitting up on the top level of the West Parking Ramp. Mighty early for customers. Who volunteers to pay them a visit?" Robin asked.

"Shouldn't you send George and Jan out there?" Joel asked. George and Jan were in the security patrol car.

"Would if I could, but they're out topping off the tank before the end of the shift. Probably scarfing down donuts too. I don't expect them back for at least another fifteen minutes, but probably more like half an hour. You know how they are. It's up to you boys."

"Yeah," Bill said. "They won't bring any back for us."

Emilio remembered how Robin had told him she had grown up with four brothers and no sisters. It explained her ability to banter with the guys and fit right in. She seemed to particularly enjoy teasing Bill, but the big guy just didn't really get it that it was because she liked him.

"I'm pretty close and on my way," Emilio said. He wondered if his girls would be up yet when he got home.

"I am going too," Joel said.

"Remember, no heroics," Robin said. "I doubt they're out there enjoying early morning lattes and donuts. Probably a drug deal going down, so they might have guns. I'm alerting the police to the suspicious activity too. Just show a presence and remember to be careful."

"Roger that," Emilio replied. "No Batman without Robin."

"Very funny," Robin groaned.

"I'm coming back to the center. My turn to be in the seat and your turn to do the walking," Bill said to Robin.

"Hoorah!"

"You're such a man, Robin," Bill teased.

"Well, somebody around here has to be," she replied.

Emilio was the first to the West Parking Ramp. He was a couple of decks down though and took to the stairs near the elevated walkway to the ramp. Too many steps to climb. His calves and buttocks burned by the time he got to the top of the ramp. He put his hands on his thighs. Too flabby. He bent over and took a moment or two to catch his breath. He patted his tummy; a little too much there too. He promised himself he would take the elevator back down when he was done up here.

"I'm just outside of the ramp now," he notified the others after having caught his breath. All he heard on his earphone was static though. He tapped the com unit on his hip, but still only static buzzed from it. Dang radio, he silently cursed the unit. He put his hands on his hips and took a few additional deep breaths before stepping forward.

Around the corner he ran into two young men, and they seemed as startled as he. He had not expected anyone to be standing there.

They spun toward him. One pulled a big silver gun out of his hoody's pocket and swung it his direction. A lightning flash lit up the parking ramp behind them. Heavy rain suddenly poured down outside, pounding the hard concrete of the parking ramp.

Emilio hands shot up to shoulder height, palms out. "Hey, man. Don't shoot. I'm just mall security. We don't carry guns, but I'm warning you real cops are on their way." Another flash of lightning lit up the parking ramp.

The two guys stared at each other, apparently unsure of what they should do. Then all the lights winked out at the same time, even the headlights of the car behind the guys. A second later, a faint wall of green light passed through all of them, only visible because it was otherwise pitch black. Another lightning flash and immediately afterward, the flash from the end of a gun barrel. Then another.

Chapter 3 – Joel

J oel had just reached the top level. Like Emilio, he
was a couple inches short of six feet. Joel,
however, was built like a stud horse. All muscle,
he looked like he was on steroids. Only he never
touched the stuff. Unlike Emilio, his face hadn't been
shaved in several days, and it was topped with straight
dark hair which hadn't been combed since the
evening before he had arrived at the mall.

Joel spoke into his mic but only static came back
through the earphone. Then everything went dark,
and two gunshot blasts echoed through the stairwell.
It was pitch black except for when the lightning lit up
the sky and everything below it. He found his
flashlight, but it flickered instead of giving a steady
beam. Banging it a few times into his other hand
didn't help. He inched forward, using the lightning
flashes to guide him.

"Emilio, you okay? Where're you at, man?" Joel
shouted.

The only response was the patter of shoes hitting
the pavement. It could not have been Emilio.

"Oh crap!" Joel muttered. He inched forward in
the dark.

Emergency lighting suddenly blinked on. He rushed forward and rounded the corner. Emilio lay on the concrete floor as tires screeched, and three cars sped away north down the ramp. Joel got a clear view of the back of the last car, a large black sedan. Caught the last number on the plate.

He rushed forward, dropped to his knees, and leaned over Emilio. "Emilio! Talk to me! Say something!"

"I ... I can't believe it. I was hit," Emilio replied. Blood seeped through Emilio's shirt. Joel ripped open the shirt. Blood gushed out of a hole in the middle of Emilio's chest. Joel press his hands down over it, trying to stop the bleeding.

"Hell, no! This can't be happening again." Joel felt a part of him wrenched back to when he crouched in a ditch over a buddy who had just taken a bullet to the chest. Ambushed along a road in Afghanistan. Nothing Joel could do for him while they waited for backup. The man bled to death as Joel helplessly watched.

"Joel, Emilio? Are you guys there? Please answer. What did you mean by it's happening again?" Robin's voice rang in his earpiece.

"You're back! Call for an ambulance. Immediately! Emilio's been shot in the chest."

"What did you mean by again?"

"Never fricking mind that. Call the dang ambulance."

"Didn't I say no heroics?"

"I don't think Emilio was trying to be a hero."

"Freaking son of a bitch! I can't call. No dang phone connection. Server … isn't connecting either. It's like I'm totally cut off from the outside world."

"What? Jeez! Emilio needs help now." Joel whipped out his cell to make the call himself for an ambulance with one hand. His other still pressed down on the wound. No reception. "What the mother … This can't be happening." He tossed his phone aside, and it clattered across the parking ramp.

He reached into Emilio's jacket and found Emilio's phone. It also indicated no reception. "Robin, I can't get any reception up here. Can you get through on yours?" He was frustrated over the lack of reception from either phone.

"Reception is always awful down here. I'll be up as fast as I can. Bill, take over the com center when you get here and call for an ambulance the instant the phone's back."

"Didn't you say you called the cops earlier?" Joel asked.

"Yeah."

"I don't hear sirens." That didn't mean they weren't on their way though.

"Emilio's been hit! Christ!" Bill shouted. "I'm coming up …"

"No," Robin interrupted. "I'm closer, and someone's always supposed to be down here." Joel knew she was breaking regs just by leaving before Bill arrived. But he believed she was making the right call.

After five minutes he heard Robin arrive. He glanced from where he now stood across the parking ramp and saw her clutching her phone as she leaned over Emilio's lifeless body. He returned to staring over the edge as he called over his shoulder, "It's too late."

"No!" She screamed. "No! No! No!" She dropped down on top of Emilio.

"I thought... hoped I wouldn't ever see this kind of thing again." Joel said. "Just a quiet mall cop job." Then his eyes caught sight of something telling him the murder of his friend wasn't his only worry.

"I've been glancing at my phone constantly on the way up. No signal. What the heck's going on?" Robin lifted a sleeve to wipe tears from her cheeks. She was not usually one to show strong emotions.

"Over here." Joel waved for her.

Eventually she rose from her knees and trudged over to his side. Her gaze followed out over the edge of the parking ramp to where he pointed. The ground below was still dark while the horizon had just started to become visible. No lights outside of the mall, except for the Ikea building just to the north of them, the headlights from a couple of cars stopped up on the overpass, and a jet which flew in a wide circle overhead. Shouts came from the direction of the cars.

Joel turned toward her. "Remember what they found down by Brown's Station last spring?"

"Heck no! That's not what's happening here." Robin shook her head.

Joel turned his gaze toward their left and pointed. "Look at 77 down there. It disappears. It's hard to see because of the dark, but the overpass seems to have been chopped off too. I think it's already happened, and we're on the wrong side of it."

Chapter 4 – Alanna

At 5:30 AM Alanna Dolencourt cruised north on Highway 77, glad for the light traffic as she came up to The Mall of America. A pickup towed a boat in front of her by a few hundred yards and the headlights of a vehicle trailed far behind her. A single car passed in the southbound lanes.

The weather seemed rather peculiar to Alanna. The forecast was supposed to be for a clear crisp autumn day with no precipitation. Instead, a few light sprinkles promptly turned into sheets of rain, and the wipers struggled to keep up clearing the windshield. Visibility had become horrible.

She was headed for Edina, a suburb to the west, to pick up a friend before they would head back down to the airport. She worried her friend would still be in bed when she got there. Something that had happened before. Alanna decided it would be wise to phone her friend, and make sure she was awake. Her phone, however, said, "Unable to complete call."

She pulled over into the left lane for the ramp to the US 494 Freeway, but her engine started to sputter. Then died. Even the headlights went out, and the wipers froze across the middle of the windshield. Even more oddly, all the overhead lamps lighting the overpass blinked out at the same time as her headlights. Somehow, she managed not to hit the concrete traffic barrier to her left as her car rolled to a stop And then she saw a faint green flash for just an instant.

The dashboard rattled and then her whole car shook with a slight rumbling. It seemed like an earthquake, but she had never felt one before, so she wasn't sure. A pair of popping sounds came from the direction of the mall. She tried to pinpoint where the sounds came from since they sounded like they might have been gunshots but it was impossible to tell in the dark. The rain stopped almost as fast as it had started. It was like the sky had snapped right back shut.

Her hands trembled as she opened the door, stepped out, and peered around. She expected darkness from overhead from all of the rainclouds, but something lit the pavement around her. She looked up. A clear full moon shined down, and then she realized stars dotted the sky in every direction she looked. She squinted as she searched. Where had all the rain come from?

The car lights flickered back on. It should have been reassuring, but it raised goosebumps on the tops of her arms instead. Everything happening around her was just too strange.

She was about to turn back toward her car when something about the road ahead caught her attention as appearing odd in the headlights' beams. She left the car door open and carefully stepped forward to investigate. Partway up the ramp, she stopped, stunned. The overpass ahead just ended in mid-air with tall trees beyond it, trees taller than the ramp itself.

Her heart pounded as she jogged back toward her car. But she stopped when she heard two cars coming up the road. Jeez! They wouldn't see the ramp was destroyed.

She waved vigorously at the oncoming headlights. Tried to get them to stop. The first car zoomed past her. Then the second. The front driver side window was down on the second one. As the car screamed past, the driver stuck his hand out and folded down all his fingers except for one.

Then the hand whipped back inside as the tires screeched. Too late. The first second car followed right behind the first and sailed off the end of the ramp.

A third car drove up the ramp, and she turned to flag it down. Waved her arms in the universal stop motion. The car slowed down.

"Stupid bitch! You're going to get yo'self freaking killed standin' on the freaking road," the driver shouted.

"Stop!" she shouted. "The ramp's out!"

The tires screeched as it skidded to a stop just short of the end of the ramp, and Alanna raced up to the driver's side.

"I tried get them to stop too, but they wouldn't. Two cars just flew over the end, and then I saw you coming." Alanna's hands shook even worse than before. "I think there was an earthquake. I felt some rumbling, although maybe that was from the ramp coming down. I don't know. But if it wasn't an earthquake, why is there a power outage? And what took down the ramp? The earthquake didn't seem strong enough that it would have caused something like that to collapse. And I don't ever recall not being able to see lights anywhere in the cities. It seems to be a blackout of the whole metropolitan area."

"Mm. Ya sure do talk a lot," the driver said.

"It's the adrenaline. Maybe some of the people in those cars down there survived. We should get down there and check. Don't you think?" Alanna breathed heavily.

"Them dudes dead," the driver said.

"We can't be sure of it. Maybe the airbags saved them, but they could be hurt and need help. We should call for an ambulance." She pulled out her cell phone as the driver put his car in reverse and quickly backed down the ramp. He seemed intent on quickly getting out of there. She turned her attention back to her phone and saw she got no signal.

"Hey! Wait!" she shouted at the car, but it did not stop. She peered around. There were no lights anywhere, except over at the mall area and a plane which flew overhead. She peered straight ahead to where the airport should be. Pitch black. No wonder the plane circled overhead, but she would have thought there would have been more than one waiting to land. How long until power came back on? Shouldn't the airport have emergency power?

She marched back to her car and searched in the glove box until she found a flashlight. She carried it back to the edge of the ramp, hoping there was a chance someone might still be alive below. Dreading that she might glimpse mangled bodies instead. Her hand on the cold wet steel railing steadied her as the dim beam of light shined over the edge.

A loud screeching noise came from below, sounding like that of metal twisting. Then a crashing sound, and she thought one of the cars must have shifted position. As she peered over the edge, careful not to lose her balance, she yelled, "Hello? Can anyone hear me down there?"

Her light reflected off the back of something huge and alive. It appeared black and enormous in the feeble small beam of her light. Large triangular spines stuck up out of a broad back that led to a thick wide head. The head was inside a car which had its rooftop ripped off. The head of an enormous dinosaur.

She screamed and dropped her flashlight. The light bounced off the concrete, over the edge, and tumbled down next to the dinosaur. She stumbled backward and fell with her rear onto the pavement. She scooted back, rose, and raced for the car.

Jeez! It just couldn't be real. She thought about what had happened down at Brown's Station. From her vantage point, it looked as though the whole area north of her had been replaced with the same terrain as down around Brown's Station. She tried the ignition and was relieved when the engine immediately started up.

A roar erupted, sounding like an eagle had screamed, only several octaves lower and magnitudes louder. The ramp itself seemed to shake from it.

She shifted the car into gear, and tires screeched as her car whipped through a U-turn. Raced back down the ramp. She headed the wrong way down the highway, and it didn't feel right. She half-expected another car to be coming up the highway, although no headlights were visible.

She took the Lindau ramp off toward the mall. But Lindau seemed to end just a few blocks ahead. She turned right at a sign that said 24th Avenue, but the road suddenly ended too after less than a block. A wide open field lay ahead and woods beyond that.

She came to a stop and stared, her mouth hanging open. Her heart had not slowed. The end of the road only meant one thing. The dinosaur didn't come to her world; she was in its world.

As her car idled, she pulled out a Castaways bar from the tray in front of the shifter. Chewing the bar, she glanced down at the other half and tossed it out her window. Screw the chocolate. She needed a bottle of tequila. A really big bottle.

Chapter 5 – Robin

R obin stood beside Joel at the edge of the parking ramp and stared out over the side just as the sun came up on the other side of the mall behind them. It was dark below them, but not so dark they couldn't see what stood there. The air didn't smell like the city anymore. Rather, it was like some mixture of compost and freshly cut grass. And it was warm already. Behind them Emilio's lifeless body lay on the concrete.

"You know where we're at, don't you?" Joel stared at the huge dinosaur below which looked like a *stegosaurus*. It had rows of plates along its broad back which appeared like shields stuck vertically into its spine, and a muscular tail behind it which ended in nine huge spikes. On the opposite end of the body, a small pointy head peacefully munched leaves off a bush.

"We're off the edge of the map, mate. Here there be monsters," Robin said, using her best imitation of Captain Barbosa's voice from the movie.

Joel sighed. *"Pirates of the Caribbean.* Now, that's a classic."

"Yeah," Robin said, "Except we're in *Jurassic Park*. We really need to speak to Spielberg right now and have him cut this scene." She joked, but inside her knots of fear had her stomach so tied up it hurt.

Joel's shoulders slumped as he turned toward Robin. "How can this be?"

She could only shake her head. She knew they were trapped. The only upside was at least she wasn't alone.

A loud screeching roar came from the direction of the overpass. The *stegosaurus* below them immediately lifted its head, turned, and ambled away in the opposite direction from the roaring noise.

Bill's voice came through their earpieces. "Something strange is going on."

"No shit," Robin replied.

"Yeah, none of the cameras on the southeast corner are working. It's all levels. Should I go check it out?" Bill asked.

"You think that's freaking strange? You need to get your butt up here and see this," Robin replied.

"See what?"

"You gotta see for yourself. If I told you, you would think I was just yanking your chain," Robin said.

"You're always doing that. But, who's going to man the center?" Bill asked.

"Just leave it and get your butt up here," she yelled. He could be so dense sometimes.

"But the regs—" Bill started.

"Forget about the stupid regs. There's no one to enforce them anymore anyway." Robin said.

"What are you talking about?" Bill asked.

"Just get the heck up here," she yelled.

Ten minutes later Bill stood with them and stared at the fleeing stegosaurus nearing the edge of the woods two hundred yards away by then. Bill was a couple inches taller than Joel. His body was like that of a farm boy, strong and stocky, but without the definition of Joel's muscles. His curly red hair was usually cut short enough to inhibit it from becoming uncontrollable. He was a little naïve sometimes, but Robin knew he wasn't stupid. Okay, not a genius, but not stupid either. He just said stupid things sometimes. It was even cute sometimes.

"This is just like what happened down in Brown's Town," Bill said.

"No shit, Sherlock!" Robin replied. "And it's Brown's Station, not Brown's Town."

"Brown's Station, Brown's Town. It could be called Brown's Shit or Shitsville. What does it matter?"

"You're such an idiot sometimes," Robin said. She was mad at him but realized she was being hard on him because of her own fears.

Bill put his hands on his hips. "Resorting to insults? That's real mature."

"We're in Shitsville," Joel muttered before she could react. They were all silent for a moment.

Then Bill turned toward them. "Dang! What are we going to we do?" There was silence for a moment as none had an immediate answer. Robin tried to think, but all she saw in her head was Emilio's face. And all she felt was a despair and a resentment toward a universe which didn't care who the victim was.

Joel cupped his ear. "Listen."

"For what?" Bill asked.

Joel scanned the sky overhead. "The plane that was circling, I don't hear it anymore. Last time I heard it, it was to the south of us. Over there." He pointed toward their left.

"Maybe they went elsewhere," Bill said.

"Is that what you think they did?" Robin asked. She decided she needed to let it go. She needed to tone it back a little to keep it from escalating into a fight and to keep her own sanity. She sucked in a deep breath. "We're all stressed," she said. Dang it if she were going to apologize though.

"Why would they circle around us for half an hour and then just leave? Where would they go?" Joel asked. "If I were flying that plane, I'd be putting it down somewhere."

"There are trees almost everywhere, except for the field over that way, and that seems a bit rough to land a plane." Robin pointed to the east.

"Yeah, and maybe too short. I bet they ditched it in the river," Joel said.

"Just like that jet did in the Hudson in that movie," Bill added. "Yeah, I know. Good movie, not a classic. What was it called?"

"I didn't hear the plane explode, and I don't see smoke," Robin said. "That's a good sign, right?"

"We should get down to the river. There're people on that plane who are going to need our help," Joel said.

"We should probably get us some weapons first though," Robin said.

"No place here to get guns," Joel said.

"Yeah, but there must be someplace with something we can use as a spear," Bill said.

"Sears has tools like pitchforks," Robin said.

"Not the Sears here," Bill said.

A thought occurred to Robin. "The Hungry Samurai!"

"The Japanese restaurant?" Joel asked.

"Yep."

Joel squinted. "We're gonna toss sushi at the dinosaurs?"

Robins chuckled. "Do you know what they have hanging right above the bar?"

"I'm guessing not a couple of chopsticks," Joel replied.

"Two samurai swords."

"I am not taking on one of those with a sword." Bill pointed in the direction the stegosaurus disappeared.

"That's a plant eater and won't bother you if you don't bother it. Probably. But what if we come across a raptor like those found down by Brown's Station?" Robin asked.

"We should get the swords," Joel said.

"What do we do with Emilio," Bill asked.

"We leave him here," Robin replied, "and help those that can still be helped." She thought it was obvious.

"No, we should drag him inside the door, so nothing can get to him. When we have time, we bury him later. It's the least we can do for him," Joel said.

She had to admit Joel was right. It wouldn't slow them down more than a minute to pull Emilio into the doorway, and she would feel awful if they found something had mutilated his body before they got back.

"That restaurant will be locked," Bill said. "I better go get the keys, so we can get in."

"That'll take a good twenty minutes to go all the way back to the center and find the right key. My car is right over at the end of this level, and I have tools in the trunk." Joel marched off toward his car.

"What kind of tools?" Bill asked.

"Tools." Joel tone suggested they should know what he meant. Bill and Robin turned to follow him across the ramp.

As Joel popped his trunk, Bill gasped. Robin turned to see what had caused the reaction.

The hotel which was supposed to be seated at the south entrance to the mall was gone. Only part of a wall with the walkway which spanned across to the second level of the mall remained. The area beyond the southeast corner of the mall was also gone. There was no crater and only a small amount of debris. Tall green stalks of grass gently waved in a light breeze where the hotel and parking ramp should have stood. It was as if those parts of the mall had never existed.

In the reality of the new world they found themselves, those parts never had.

Chapter 6 – DeJuan

It appeared the pilots' effort to ditch the plane was going to work as the plane skimmed along the surface and lost speed like a flat stone skipping over the lake, but then they hit something. Something big.

The front of the plane came up,. but it did not have the speed to rise. With no lift under its wings, the big airliner nose-dived back into the lake. The back of the plane swung around nearly 180 degrees before it came to a sudden and complete stop, Inside, DeJuan felt as if he had been picked up and body slammed.

After all motion had stopped, the floor angled downward slightly toward the front and the left of the plane; that direction pointed toward a deeper section of the lake. Luckily, the plane had lost most of its momentum by the time of the nosedive, and the plane survived mostly intact.

DeJuan blinked a few times and then breathed a huge sigh of relief once he realized the plane no longer moved. He was still alive. At least for now.

He glanced around at the other passengers. Two men rubbed what appeared to be big goose eggs on their foreheads, and a woman appeared to have something wrong with her arm or shoulder. DeJuan didn't have time to figure out if it was a broken arm, a separated shoulder, or just a sprain. Two of the attendants already headed to those injured anyway.

DeJuan worried about the pilots. Another man must have had the same thoughts; they both rushed forward to the door to the flight deck. They pulled and yanked on the handle together but couldn't budge the locked door. They banged their fists on its solid surface. Against the metal. No answer. DeJuan searched around for a bar of any sort to pry the door but didn't spot anything useful.

The tall attendant, Freeda, opened the front hatch near them, and stagnant lake water suddenly rushed in. She was swept back up against DeJuan and the other man by the incoming flow. The three of them, drenched, pushed back toward the hatch, but the force from the incoming lake water was too great. They were forced back toward the rear of the plane as the level quickly rose above the hatch door. Soon the front filled with lake water. Duckweed, tiny floating plants, gave the appearance of a green mat on top of the water. DeJuan banged his hand up against the overhead and swore; they were abandoning the pilots. He saw no way to help them though.

While the three of them were in the front, the other passengers and attendants had opened an emergency exit and filed out, one at a time, onto the wing pointed toward the nearby shore.

DeJuan, along with Freeda and the other man who attempted to rescue the pilots, followed behind the last of the passengers who exited the plane. Freeda carefully stepped through the hatch out onto the wing ahead of DeJuan. Her head darted around at the world around them. DeJuan eyes darted around as well as he stepped gingerly behind her toward the end of the wing, careful not to slip on the wet metal surface. Those in front of them slid off the edge of the wing and landed in three feet of water. The flotation devices were not actually needed, and they weren't going to be useful for defense against predators either. DeJuan loosened the one around his neck and flung it onto the shore after sliding into the water.

The other man who had helped in the attempt to open the door to the pilots was the last one to leave the plane. As DeJuan stepped onto dry land, he turned to lend a hand to Freeda whose shoe stuck in the mud where the lake met the shore. At the same time, he saw the last man slide off the wing and splash into the lake.

As soon as the man's feet hit the bottom, his legs were pulled out from under him. He screamed and thrashed his arms as something had gripped onto his legs.

DeJuan tugged hard on Freeda's arm. The two fell backward onto the shore.

The man disappeared under the surface of the lake. His head and an arm reappeared but were then pulled back under again. A long thick tail broke the surface as whatever monster had grabbed the man appeared to be taking him to the bottom. The tail disappeared too, and then all that was left were swirling waves and a hole in the matt of duckweed.

It appeared to DeJuan to have been an alligator or crocodile, but he wasn't sure; it could have been almost anything. Maybe another type of dinosaur.

It all happened so fast nobody had even barely moved before the man was gone. Dragged to his doom. One of the flight attendants stared at the lake and screamed at the top of her lungs until the other attendant put her arm around the woman and tugged her away from the water's edge. People scrambled up the steep bank as they tried to get far away from the monster before it or another like it returned.

"What was that? Anybody get a good look at it?" DeJuan asked. Nobody else saw more than the tail either.

After a minute of climbing, DeJuan stopped on the side of the slope and gazed down on the plane whose nose was under water in a long sliver of a lake that was once a part of the river.

It didn't seem fair. Those who helped get them down safely were drowned, and the other man who tried to save the pilots was killed by a monster. If they hadn't attempted to save the pilots, there was chance the last man would have safely made it ashore before the monster had come. The captain's last name was Thormson; DeJuan knew from the name tag on the captain's jacket. The captain had kept his promise of ensuring all the passengers stepped off the plane. But

DeJuan didn't know the names of the other pilot or the man dragged under. They had all died heroically, and he didn't even know their names. Maybe he could find out from the attendants or other passengers. It somehow seemed important.

A large dinosaur thrashed around out in the lake several hundred yards up from the plane. People above DeJuan were spooked even further by it and pushed harder to get to the trees covering the plateau a hundred feet above the lake. The dinosaur stopped thrashing and disappeared under the lake. It appeared to have been what the biologists had designated a *Brownstasaurus*, usually referred to as a bronto by most people. That was what the plane must have hit, but now the dinosaur was gone. Probably died from the damage caused by the glancing blow it took from the plane. It was not the type of dinosaur DeJuan worried about though.

Above him, the Wanderluchs squabbled. DeJuan had caught their names while the plane had circled, but they were otherwise strangers to him. Everyone around was.

June stomped down hard. "This climb's so darn steep. Why can't you ever help me?"

"I help you all the dang time," Jack, her husband, yelled.

"Well, you're not helping me now," June said.

"What do you want me to do? Carry you? You know how my back is," Jack said.

"Give me your hand. You can do that, can't you? You don't want me to slip on the rocks or trip over these stupid roots, do you?" she yelled. "They're everywhere. Why do trees need so many darn roots anyway? I was not made for walking in a wilderness like this."

By then DeJuan caught up to them. He whispered through clenched teeth. "What do you two think? We're in some kind of park here? This is not freakin' Central Park. Think *Jurassic Park* instead. Pipe down, or you two are going to get the rest of us killed."

"Stick up for me, Jack. The man's yelling at me, and I don't like it," June whispered. "Not one bit."

"I'm not yelling. And if you don't shut up, you might just become a meal for a dinosaur yourself," DeJuan whispered.

June scowled, but she kept quiet after that. Jack didn't say anything and actually smiled at DeJuan. Did the man like the thought of her being eaten by a dinosaur? Maybe he just liked that she was now quiet.

DeJuan's thoughts returned to the pilots, heroes in his mind. They were in the front part of the plane where it was the most dangerous, and they had gotten everyone else down safely just as the captain had promised, but they had died in the process. Would the rest of them survive to benefit from the pilots' sacrifice? They had to get to the mall. That was their only chance.

Once everyone had reached the top, they headed in a northerly direction. Easy to know the direction as the early morning sun was rising due east from them. The comfortable early morning temperature probably meant it was going to be unbearably hot later. They hiked on what appeared to be a trail for a while, but then they veered off when the trail turned toward the west. The hike alternated between easy and hard. Sometimes they traipsed across open forest floor, and then sometimes they crawled through low-lying brush which snagged their clothes and scratched their arms and necks.

DeJuan shook his head. The group made such a racket in the woods. Was everyone so incapable of lifting their feet so the leaves wouldn't rustle? Or avoid snapping all the twigs? If he hadn't been so concerned about staying quiet, he would have yelled to the group that they missed a couple of sticks.

DeJuan wondered if they were anywhere near the mall when he heard a crackling in the bushes behind them. He spun around but couldn't spot anything in the thick undergrowth. He was at the very end of the group, so there should have been no one behind him. Maybe the pilots had made it out after all and trailed them. He hoped but didn't think it likely. The pilots wouldn't have stopped and remained hidden just because he turned around.

The lush bushes were so thick in places it could have hidden a freight train. Something was out there, and he had nothing for protection. He glanced around and spotted a relatively straight dead branch on the forest floor not far away. He picked it up and snapped off a side branch, so he was left with a relatively straight six-foot long stick about as thick as his wrist. He peered back but still couldn't see what hid in the bushes, so he turned to catch up with the rest of the group.

His shoe caught on something, a root or branch, and he almost stumbled before catching his balance. As he glanced down, he saw something on the ground. Light yellow in color in contrast to the dark hues of the rest of the woodland floor. He leaned over to pull it out of the ground and then examined what was in his hand.

"What is it?" Freeda asked.

"Yikes!" DeJuan jerked upright as he held out the object. "You freaking scared the bejesus out of me."

The attendant gasped and pointed at what he held. "Is that a tooth?"

"Uh-ha. It's why you gave me such a scare. Combined with what's back there. Something's in those woods." DeJuan pointed back toward the path they had made.

"Something's back there? What?" Freeda's eyes sprung large.

"Heck if I know. But I hope he's not looking for his missing tooth," DeJuan replied.

"We need to get the heck out of here," Freeda said.

"Right behind you. Go!"

They hurried to catch up to the rest of the group. DeJuan constantly glanced over his shoulder, wondering if some beast were about to rush out from the bushes behind him.

As the people ahead of him passed a particularly thick brushy area and stepped into a clearing, they all stopped. Something was going on up ahead. Again,

DeJuan heard the rustling of leaves somewhere behind them, but he still couldn't make out what lurked back there. He hoped not to find out.

Voices came from ahead. He and Freeda finally caught up with the group as they stood in waist high green grass just past the edge of the woods.

Chapter 7 - Robin

Bill had stayed back to warn all the other night workers in the mall. Besides, they all agreed it would be unwise to go out without a weapon, and there were only two swords. Robin had claimed one by her knowledge of them. Joel grabbed the other, and Bill was not about to argue with him over it.

Robin and Joel hiked across an open field to the south of the mall toward where they thought the plane most likely had gone down. As they neared the end of the field, several of the survivors from the plane stepped out from the edge of the woods. Most in the group were badly out of shape and winded from their hike through the woods.

Joel directed the band, consisting of people in a broad age range of twenties to upper sixties, to take shelter in the mall. Robin was thankful there were no small children. One man, who introduced himself as a priest, and three flight attendants assisted those who struggled to keep up as the plane's survivors dragged themselves across the field. Robin noticed the last man, a tall black man, had not yet moved. He still peered back into the brush.

"What you lookin' at? Is someone still back there who fell behind?" she asked.

The man did not take his eyes off the brush. "No, I think we were being stalked by something. I couldn't see it, but I've been hearing its movements for a while now."

Robin glanced at Joel as she gripped tighter onto the sword in her hands.

"You sure?" Robin peered into the woods.

"No. But I've been hearing leaves rustling behind us for the last ten, maybe fifteen, minutes."

"I think whatever's out there will be more likely to attack us if our backs are turned, so let's not show our backs. We walk backwards toward the mall," Joel said.

That strategy worked for about thirty feet, but then a monster slowly stepped out from the brush. It was big, maybe eight feet tall and fifteen to twenty feet long. The beast flashed rows of long, yellow-stained teeth as it took a step toward them. Then another step.

"That's one big, son of a bitchin' raptor." Robin boosted her sword out higher in front of her and stepped backwards.

"This isn't a raptor. It's a juvenile *Minneasarus rex*. An *M. rex*." DeJuan held his stick out in defense. The rex slowly closed the gap between them. "What the hell do we do?"

"Shit, I don't know," Robin replied.

"I think I already did that," the man said.

Robin had to give him credit for having displayed a sense of humor while under pressure. The rex poked its head forward, and the man shoved his stick at it. The rex snapped down on it and tore it out of the man's arms with a jerk of its head. The end of the stick splintered in the jaws of the rex as if it were a mere toothpick.

The man scurried behind Robin and Joel for protection as the three stepped backwards. The rex matched their pace but needed far fewer steps than them.

It was only a matter of when it would strike. The swords might hurt it, but that would be little consolation if the rex killed one of them.

Then a deafening rumbling blast of a roar came from their right, and Robin peeked toward where the roar had come from. Another rex trotted toward them. It made the one in front of them seem like a midget.

"Ah, crap!" she cursed. As if one rex wasn't enough for them. Now they would have to contend with Junior and his dad. It appeared hopeless.

However, the rex in front of them gave a snort in the direction of larger rex, turned, and then trotted back into the brush instead of attacking them.

The three of them wasted no time. The odds were not good for them defending against the smaller rex, but they had absolutely no chance against the larger one.

They turned and dashed as fast they could toward the mall. Followed the trail already made by the other passengers through the tall grass. Ahead, Robin saw most of the other passengers neared the mall already. Over her shoulder, she saw the larger rex turn toward the brush instead toward them. A series of tremendous screeching roars were bellowed out into the woods. The bigger one warned Junior this was Daddy's hunting grounds, and Junior wasn't welcome.

Only then, after the big rex secured its dominance, did it turn around and race after them. The time lag gave the trio a head start, and they certainly needed it. Robin hoped it was going to be enough.

They raced on, and her legs soon burned with each step. She glanced back. The rex gained on them, but it appeared they would reach the mall before the rex caught up. But would it stop just because they reached the mall?

Someone held the door open for them on the Macy's corner of the mall. Thankfully, Bill had gotten the message out to the staff. When she had left the mall with Joel, they had departed through the opening to the southeast. If they returned through that same hole, the rex would likely follow them right inside.

They caught up to June and her husband just as they reached the door. One of the night custodians held the door open for them but stared, dumbstruck, at the oncoming rex. Robin was the last to reach the door. She grabbed onto the arm of the man who held the door and jerked him inside.

"Everyone, hide!" Joel yelled. Bodies ducked behind counters and clothes racks.

Robin dove behind a clothes rack and peeked between evening dresses as a lady knelt on the floor next to her and softly mumbled a prayer. Robin reached down and gently put a finger over the lady's mouth. The lady looked up at her with big eyes but kept quiet.

The rex slowed and strutted up to the large glass walls. Up close, Robin realized how truly gigantic the creature was. The monster stopped, its nostrils very slowly drifted toward the glass, and the rex snorted. A circle of fog covered the glass around the nostrils before they gently banged into the window. The pane crackled and then shattered.

But the pane was safety glass and the snout did not push through. It seemed that the rex had not expected the resistance from the window because the giant pulled its head away from the glass, but it stayed and stared at the vast racks of clothing for a minute. Its snort, sort of like that of a horse, could be heard even through the glass barrier. After another minute, the beast turned and marched toward the east around the mall.

Joel crept up to the window. "It's gone, at least for now. Is anyone hurt?"

"There's someone over here on the floor," one of the passengers shouted. "He's got a hand over his chest. Oh my God! I think he's having a heart attack."

The tall flight attendant turned to the tall black man. "Dr. Jazkins, he needs your help."

"Me?" Dr. Jazkins appeared confused.

"On the plane, you said you're a doctor," the flight attendant said.

"You're a doctor?" Robin asked.

"You are. Aren't you?" the attendant asked. "I hope you weren't lying."

"No, but I'm not that kind of doctor. I am the Ph.D. kind." Dr. Jazkins spelled it out. "I study medicinal properties of plants."

Robin realized Dr. Jazkins was not going to be of help. She rushed to the heart attack victim herself, and Joel arrived there about the same time.

People crowded around the downed man. "We're trained in CPR. Give us room," Robin shouted.

The man was motionless. Not even his chest moved. Robin put her head on the man's chest.

"No heartbeat," she said to Joel who kneeled across the man's body from her.

"I got his chest," he said. "Give him air."

Joel put his hands on the man's chest and pumped as Robin scooted over, put her lips over the man's mouth, squeezed his nose, and blew air into him. Everyone else stood around and watched in anxious silence. Occasionally, they glanced out the window for the rex.

After five minutes, Joel put his head down to the man's chest for a short bit before coming back up and sighing. "He's gone." He rose to his feet. "He's not coming back."

Robin put her hands on her hips. She was still on her knees, but she knew Joel was right, and she was exhausted.

The priest came forward. "We should pray for his safe passage." He knelt before the body of the man. "O' Lord, every man has a purpose that you give to him in life. This man's life on Earth, or wherever this place is, has now ended, and so has his purpose. I don't know what kind of life he led; only you can be his judge. Eternal rest grant unto him, O' Lord, and let perpetual light shine upon him. May he rest in peace. Amen."

"Amen," others murmured.

"Bill, are you there?" Robin asked into her mic.

"Yeah, I'm here. Did you find them?"

"Yeah. One man just died of a heart attack though. We attempted CPR on him, but his heart had given up. We just couldn't get him back. The pilots did not come with them, and they said another man was killed by a crocodile or something. The rest are safe with us. We're holed up in Macy's. A big dinosaur that looked like a *T. Rex* chased us into here, but it's gone now."

"How many are with you?" Bill asked.

"Sixteen alive from the plane, not counting the guy who had the heart attack. Plus two from the night staff, Joel and myself."

"There are 16 accounted for from the night cleaning staff then. That makes 36, counting ourselves, we know about that are here."

"You might want to check your math again, genius," Robin said. "It's 35."

"Oh, yeah. There are only three of us now." There was sorrow in his voice.

Robin immediately regretted correcting him. "It's hard to believe he's gone."

"Are there any more people who might be here?" Joel asked.

"There are five on the night custodial staff still not accounted for," Bill answered. "They may have left the premises. I'm rolling back the video files now. Hey, what the …"

"What's going on?" Robin asked. "Bill, talk to me!"

A man's scream came from somewhere in the mall.

"A big dinosaur's in the mall. I think it might be the one that chased you. It just … oh, my God … it's horrible," Bill yelled.

"Talk to me, Bill," Joel said.

"It … It just snatched up a man and is eating him. Argh! I can't stand to watch. You should get out of there. That monster is just down the hall from you."

"How did it get in?" the tall flight attendant asked.

"The southeast corner of the mall is gone. It's a wide-open hole there now," Joel replied. "Does anyone know if the mall entrance to this store is open?"

A man who wore a custodial uniform answered with a Mexican accent, "The gate's down." He was the man who had unlocked the front door and held door for them.

"Just the grill?" Joel asked.

"Si. Yes."

"That won't be enough to even slow it down," Robin said. "We may be having a visitor soon."

"Up the escalators, now," Joel shouted. The up and down escalators were opposite each other and stood still. They had become steps.

People jumped as they heard loud clinking from the metal grille gate and then crashing noises as it was destroyed. Robin thought all their talking and noise probably alerted the monster to their location. It might have been able to sniff them out anyway though.

Robin jumped toward the nearest escalator. So did everyone else. People pushed against each other in a frenzy to get up to safety. Someone screamed, alerting the rex exactly to where to find its next meal.

The steps on the escalator were vertically uneven, unlike real stairs. A woman tripped at the bottom, creating a bottleneck. People jumped over her. After the man in front of Robin jumped over the woman, Robin stopped and pulled the woman to her feet.

Robin noticed the lady's skirt didn't give her legs protection, and her knee was cut from the fall. Someone squeezed around them and knocked the lady back down again.

Robin cursed, turned her head, and spotted the rex inside the store. It stomped their direction.

The monstrous head knocked over racks of clothing and handbags. Its arms were comparable to a human arm but appeared tiny on the huge body of the rex. The arms were about height of the clothes racks though. One caught a white fashion purse, all covered with rhinestones. It carried the purse as it advanced toward them which would have been comical had the danger not been so great. The purse caught on another rack and was ripped away. The rex in the mall was so much bigger than the juvenile stalker. Teeth, head, everything was up sized.

The rex stopped and swiveled its head toward the dead man who lay on the floor as Robin yanked the woman back to her feet. They scrambled up the escalator behind the others. Robin didn't look back until they reached the top. The dead man's body had saved their lives. The priest had been wrong. The man's body had served one last purpose. Robin felt a pang of guilt over being thankful for the dead man but understood they couldn't have brought the man's body with them anyway once the rex had entered the mall.

Robin glanced around as reached the top of the escalator. People already climbed the next set of escalators to the third floor, putting extra distance between them and the terrifying creature below.

Everyone, other than the heart attack victim, made it safely up to the third floor with no more than minor scrapes and bruises. Robin examined the woman she had helped, but her cuts were only minor. Robin thought it was a major miracle they all made it up safely, considering the chaos of the scramble.

At Joel's request, the custodian opened the front sliding grill gate. Robin followed Joel and Dr. Jazkins out onto the walkway, and they peered over the edge at the central amusement park area.

"You don't think that monster could climb up the escalators out here, do you?" Robin kept glancing up and down the walkway. "These escalators are wider than those in Macy's."

"I doubt it," the tall black man said. "They're still way too narrow for that creature, but smaller dinosaurs like the *Wiscoraptor* probably could."

"Whisker-raptors? Are those the Jurassic Park-like dinosaurs?" Robin asked.

"*Wiscoraptors* are the raptorsaurs. Yeah."

"How is it that you know all this stuff, Dr. Jazkins?" she asked. "What is it you do for a living? Or are you just big into dinosaurs?"

"You can just call me DeJuan. I work for a pharmaceutical company out in the bay area, and I was *supposed* to be on a connecting flight down to La Crosse this morning. Plan was to meet up with a botanist, John del May, to collect plant and soil samples from the Brown's Station Zone to take back to our company. I studied up as much as I could about the dinosaurs I might run … might have run into down there."

"The dirt from there might be valuable?"

"You would be surprised how many drugs came from microorganisms in soil."

"So, you're a science geek," Robin said. "I wouldn't have guessed." She was impressed. She took some science classes back in high school and passed, barely, but didn't remember any of it.

He stared at her. "Why? Because I'm black?"

She turned and looked him in the eye. Did she just offend him? "No! No! Because of the way you're dressed. Come on! Blue jeans and t-shirt?"

He relaxed a bit and turned toward the view below. "You think all scientists go running around in white lab coats everywhere when they're not in the lab?"

Robin always hated to say sorry and usually found other words. "I suppose not. Guess that makes sense. Mm. Guess it also means you must be pretty smart."

"Hmph. Not smart enough to know how to get out of this dang mess."

"Shh! Below us." Joel whispered. He pointed down. The rex emerged out into the central court area. It snorted, and then craned its enormous head and stared up at them with its huge baseball sized eyes.

"I wonder why their heads are so big. They are proportionally bigger than a *T. rex*'s," DeJuan muttered. "And the *T. rex* had an enormous head itself."

The rex craned its head away and stomped across the park with slow huge strides until he was at the Lego store entrance. There it stopped. Let out monstrous roars twice up at the giant, multi-colored, Lego-constructed saber-toothed tiger and caveman up on the roof. The rex then snorted several times. Then it stomped toward the south walkway.

"I wonder what it would have done if the Lego Store still had its dinosaurs up instead of the tiger and the cave dude," Joel said.

"Mm. Maybe it would depend on if they were boy dinosaurs or girl dinosaurs," Robin said.

Chapter 8 - DeJuan

It was late morning, and most of the people were up on the south-side third level food court. DeJuan sat at the same table as the three security guards. Across from him, Bill's head lay flat on the table. As he peered around, DeJuan noticed many of the mall workers rested, having not slept all night. He glanced down at the empty cups of yogurt and banana skins in front of him and was thankful Joel had cut open entrances to a couple of the fast-food shops around the food court. At least they had food and bottled water for now.

DeJuan peered around. He spotted the night workers, easy to identify because of their uniforms. And the fifteen other survivors from the plane. There was one other, a woman in blue jeans and a blouse, seated alone at a table. He didn't remember her from the plane, and he was sure he would have noticed a woman as pretty as her. Tall and thin with wavy blond hair and perfect complexion.

"Either of you know that woman over there?" DeJuan asked Robin and Joel. "I'm sure she wasn't on the plane."

Robin shook her head, but Joel stared for a few seconds before he answered. "Yeah, I do know who she is."

He got up and walked toward her. DeJuan and Robin followed a few steps behind. "Hello. You're Alanna Dolencourt. Aren't you? From *Wake Up, Cities*," Joel said.

"Uh, yeah. That's me. Guilty as charged."

"Everyone else here either works here or was on the plane that went down. I'm guessing you were driving up the highway when the change happened."

"Yeah, I thought it was obvious." She placed her empty juice container on the foam plate in front of her.

"May I?" Joel pointed at the seat opposite her. "My name's Joel Axel." He then introduced the others.

She waved at the seats around the table, an invitation for them to sit. "You all watch my show?" Her eyes danced around between the three of them.

DeJuan shook his head and saw Robin do the same as they took seats. But Joe replied, "Sometimes I catch it before going to sleep in the morning."

She nodded. "May I ask some questions?" After Joel nodded, she asked, "I assume this is just like what happened at Brown's Station. Would you all agree?"

"Except, it is a much smaller area that got this ... you know, affected," DeJuan answered. "I don't know what to call this phenomenon."

"I'm calling it poofing," Alanna said.

"Poofing?" DeJuan squinted. It didn't seem like a scientific or professional term to him. It did seem to fit the experience though.

"Yeah, like one instant you're driving down the highway and then poof, the next you're down the rabbit hole and in Alice's land. What we call it though is just semantics," Alanna replied. "My cell is not getting any reception. I assume that we lost all contact with the outside."

"Yeah, we're on our own, sister," Robin agreed.

"Is this everybody here?"

"As far as we know," Joel replied.

"What about outside of the mall?"

"Outside?" Joel squinted.

"The Ikea building out there. Could there be people over there?"

Joel and Robin exchanged glances. "We hadn't thought about it, but maybe we should check it out," Robin said. "The more the merrier for this party."

"Glad someone's enjoying this." DeJuan eyed Robin.

"Moping about what happened to us won't do any good is the way I look at it," Robin said.

"No one is rescuing us. Are they?" Alanna asked.

"No," Joel said. "We're on our own."

"Was afraid you'd say that," Alanna sighed. "One more question. Where can a girl get a bottle of tequila around here?"

"Later we'll share a bottle," Joel replied. "But first we have a job to do."

Robin turned to DeJuan. "Maybe you would like to come with us to check out Ikea. It could be a fun little adventure."

"Um ... Yeah, if there's any way I can help. Don't know about your definition of fun though." It sounded less like an adventure and more like going in and freeing hostages from some terrorists. Only the terrorists were bigger than typical and ate their hostages and the rescuers. But if there were people over there who needed help, he felt he should try.

"We need to get you a weapon a little better than a stick this time," Joel said.

"You wouldn't have another of those swords?" DeJuan would rather have had a gun but knew it was too much to hope for since he hadn't seen the others carrying them. A sword would be probably the best he could hope for.

"Sorry! These are the only two," Robin replied.

"There are small axes in the fire boxes," Joel said.

"I'd prefer something with a bit of a longer reach. Maybe a spear," DeJuan said.

"I don't think there're any spears in the mall," Robin said.

"Maybe we can make a few," Joel said. "We can use a knife for a sharp point, and I'm sure we can find something for a shaft. I saw knives over at Macy's when we were there."

"Bill's gonna need one too," Robin said.

"Should we wake him?" Joel asked.

"Nah. The baby needs his sleep," Robin said. "We can wake him before we head over to Ikea 'cause I'm sure he won't want to miss out on all the fun."

DeJuan noticed that Robin seemed to pick on Bill. Was there something between them? And did she really think this was going to be fun? Must have been sarcasm.

An hour later DeJuan stood with the three security guards inside the main north side entrance of the mall. He knew he was out his element on the mission. Questioned why he agreed to come along. He was at home in a lab holding a beaker and not outside fighting some dinosaur with a spear. "Is there a plan?"

"We go there. We get anybody there out. We come back here alive," Joel said.

DeJuan frowned. "Sounds like we're winging it."

"Yeah, we're winging it," Robin said.

Joel squinted as he surveyed the areas both to the left and the right. "All right, let's move out."

He opened the door, and the rest followed him out into the bright sunshine of a noon sun. It was especially hot outside for an autumn day. They slowly marched out on the mall entrance road to where it intersected with Lindau. DeJuan kept glancing around everywhere but didn't spot any dinosaurs. They marched across Lindau at a faster pace until they came to a stand of fifteen-foot fir trees which lined the opposite corner. Joel crouched behind the trees, and everyone else followed his example.

DeJuan leaned on his make-shift spear, fashioned from a long curtain rod crimped on one end until the handle of a four-inch paring knife could fit into it. It was secured there with duct tape. Lots of duct tape. Bill held a nearly identical spear. "There're three cars in the lot." There might have been more they couldn't see from where they hid.

Joel nodded. "So there's a good chance of people inside."

"Or were inside," Robin said.

Joel looked at her before glancing at Bill and DeJuan. "We're going to start at the entrance under the parking ramp. Keep your eyes peeled for any unfriendlies in the shadows."

Again, Joel led. He trotted forward toward the huge, blue and yellow, elevated block of a building and then slowed as he approached the parking area at ground level. A glass-sided entrance housed escalators leading up to the shopping areas above. DeJuan squinted, trying to spot anything hidden on the dark opposite side of the entrance area.

They eased up to the glass-sided structure. Joel's right hand shot up, and everyone froze. He stood still as a statue, peering into the interior. DeJuan searched for movement. Any strange shadows. Wondered what had spooked Joel. After a while Robin slid up to Joel's side.

"What is it?" she whispered.

"Across the other side," he whispered.

DeJuan slowly eased forward behind the two. The glass on the opposite side had a big section smashed inward.

Joel leaned against the glass. "I don't see anything moving, so whatever did this is probably gone now. Let's go in over there through the hole. It'll save us the time of having to cut through the lock. Keep alert though." As if he needed to remind everyone of it. He eased toward his left and led slowly around the entrance structure, and then he peeked around the corner for a minute.

He stepped around and waved for everyone else to follow. The opening was only a few steps away. A large whooshing noise suddenly came from their left.

DeJuan thrust his spear out in the direction. A flock of pigeons flew out from under the parking area.

He lowered his spear and peaked at the others. Embarrassed. Spooked by dang pigeons. What was he going to do when he faced real danger? He noticed Bill and Robin had their weapons raised too, and it made him feel a little better.

"That scared the shit out of me," Bill said.

"Do you mean—" Robin teased.

Bill interjected, "Just a figure of speech."

Joel leaned against the glass still in place in the structure and stared down at the hole. "Looks like this was done by a rex or other large animal, but it's too small for a rex to go through. We shouldn't assume other dinosaurs haven't gone in though." Joel stepped carefully through the opening.

DeJuan followed behind him. Their shoes made scrunching noises as they tiptoed across a sheet of smashed safety glass. The sound seemed very loud, announcing their presence/ in the otherwise quiet building. Joel held his sword pointed out and silently climbed up the steps of the escalator to the first floor. Just like at the mall, the escalator stood unmoving, but an emergency generator kept the interior softly lit.

Joel reached the first floor and waited for everyone else to catch up. To the left, a hallway led to the checkout stations. Ahead, another escalator led to the second floor. He crept up to the next escalator and again climbed.

Once on the second floor, he again waited for the others to catch up. A cafeteria was to the left, and to the right was an aisle lined on both sides with open rooms decorated to resemble functional living rooms. Windows surrounded the cafeteria brightening that area.

Joel stepped off toward the windows and then froze. Everyone else froze too. DeJuan peered around the building for a period and wondered what had gotten the man's attention this time. The tension was so nerve-racking DeJuan thought he could smell it. Or perhaps what he smelled was his own body odor from being nervous. Was this what people meant by the smell of fear?

Robin eased up to Joel and whispered in his ear. Joel pointed ahead to where two small red streaks stained the floor. After a pause, Joel slowly stepped toward the streaks. He squatted, ran a finger over one of the streaks, and raised his finger to his face to examine it. Ahead, more streaks pointed forward.

The group followed the trail until they came to a set of restrooms. In front of the men's entrance, lay the remains of a man's body. DeJuan stared for a few seconds and then realized the spear in his hand quivered. He had never seen a mutilated body before.

The others moved forward, and he followed. The man was a bloody mess, and the stomach and chest cavity had been emptied. DeJuan had to turn his gaze away.

"I'm gonna be sick!" Bill spun and heaved off to the side.

DeJuan's stomach wasn't well either—the odor of Bill's meal didn't help. He took a couple of deep breaths. After a few seconds, he felt a little better.

Where was the creature that killed the man? It seem unlikely a predator would leave its prey after making the kill. After a minute Bill regained control of his stomach.

"Are you all okay?" Joel asked.

Bill and Robin nodded, and DeJuan said he was okay. Unlike the rest of them, Joel appeared calm and unaffected by what lay in front of them. He squatted by the body and examined it. He reached into the man's pockets and pulled out a wallet and fingered through it until he found an identification card.

"I'm going to check out the inside of the restrooms," Joel said. "Keep a sharp eye out." He disappeared for a minute and then reappeared only to disappear into the second one. He returned and reported the restrooms were empty.

"What do we do with the body?" DeJuan asked.

"Nothing for now. It's more important to find out if anyone's still alive in here."

"Okay." DeJuan nervously nodded as he accepted the logic. He noticed, though, how Joel seemed unfazed by everything they had seen so far.

"Which way?" Joel pointed his finger back and forth between the cafeteria and the living room showrooms.

"Um. We're at Ikea. We should follow the arrows," Robin's toe tapped one of the arrows on the floor near her. Faux living rooms lined the walkway in the direction she chose.

Joel nodded. "As good a direction as any." Then he crept past her toward the first couch as his blade rested on his right shoulder, both hands on the handle.

As he passed a couch, DeJuan put out a hand and rubbed it across the fabric. The soft sensation of the texture helped him sense the reality of room and made it seem less surreal.

"Wha!" DeJuan grunted as he spun and pointed his spear toward the left.

Joel halted and then slowly drew back to him. "What is it?" he whispered. Joel stared out where DeJuan's spear pointed.

"I thought I heard something over there," DeJuan whispered. Sweat beaded on his brow. The feeling was familiar like when they were in the woods after they had abandoned the plane, and they were being stalked.

"Something?" Joel asked.

DeJuan realized he should have been more specific. "Yeah, a faint clicking noise."

"But you didn't see anything."

DeJuan shook his head. He couldn't hear the sound anymore either.

After a while, Joel whispered, "Let's keep moving. Keep a close eye on our rear though. I don't want anything sneaking up on our asses. Keep quiet and we'll get them bastards."

DeJuan squinted. "I'm confused. Are we hunting them now?" he whispered.

"What's confusing?" Joel whispered.

"I thought they were hunting us."

"The best defense is a good offense." Joel turned and stalked forward again. DeJuan thought the man was possibly a little bit nuts. Nevertheless, DeJuan followed behind him. He certainly wasn't going to turn around and go back alone.

They continued past wall units. Then they wound around past kitchens and dining rooms. DeJuan was sure he heard the clicking sound again, like that of a dog walking on a hard floor with nails that needed trimming. The team wound past the desks and workspace designs and came up to bedroom designs.

"Did you see that?" Bill asked as he turned to look in DeJuan and Joel's direction and then frowned. "Dammit! Where is Joel?" he whispered.

DeJuan spun around to where Joel had been just a moment before, but he was gone. Had vanished. It was like in those horror movies where they just silently picked off people one by one. But DeJuan counted on Joel to lead them in the place—even if he was a little nuts. The man couldn't be the first to be picked off. Could he? DeJuan's heart raced even harder. What chance did it leave for the rest of them?

"What did you see?" Robin whispered.

"A big lizard tail, but it disappeared behind that stack over there." Bill pointed. "Where the heck's Joel?"

"He was in front of DeJuan a second ago," Robin whispered. Everyone's eyes darted around, but there was no clue about what might have happened to Joel.

"Dammit, Joel!" DeJuan whispered a little too loud. An instant later, a loud clicking sound echoed around them. A flash of movement. A raptor charged straight at him from where Bill had seen the tail.

He stared into the beady eyes locked on him. A scream came from somewhere. Then he realized it came from his own mouth.

The creature was almost on him. Somehow his spear found its way to stick out in front of himself. The creature impaled itself on it up to the duct tape. His shoes slid as he held stiffly to his spear. The spear hit a rib and sliced off to the left.

The raptor halted. DeJuan grunted as he instinctively thrusted hard on the spear, and it went clear through the other side of the raptor.

A second raptor let out a screech, and DeJuan screamed. It charged at them from his right side.

He tugged on his spear. But it was yanked out from his hands as the impaled raptor spun. Ran the other direction with the spear still sticking through him.

DeJuan held up two empty arms. Robin and Bill were on the other side of him. Too far to reach him before the raptor sank its teeth and claws into him.

DeJuan turned his head toward the attacking creature. He stared at the charging monster. Sure he was about to die. Everything seemed to happen in slow motion.

Then a sword shot out from behind a stack of pillows. The raptor's head rolled off to the side. The headless body bowled into DeJuan, knocking him to the floor. Blood gushed onto his shirt and jeans.

Meanwhile, the impaled raptor ran through an opening between two sections, only the ends of the spear caught. Put an end to the creature's forward progress. It dropped onto the floor on its back. Only its legs twitched.

Bill ran up to it and jabbed down several times with his spear to make sure it was dead and then opened his mouth wide. A primal scream echoed through the building. "You want a piece of us? You want a piece of us?" he yelled.

DeJuan hastily pushed the body of the dead raptor off his legs and scrambled to his feet. Heart pounding, he glanced around for other raptors. There were none. He scrambled over next to Bill to retrieve his spear, but the rod was badly bent in two places.

He tried to straighten it before he pulled it out of the raptor's body, but the rod snapped into two pieces instead.

"Shit! What do I do?" DeJuan felt defenseless.

Joel looked around and pulled a curtain rod down out of one of the display bedrooms. "This one is shorter, but we can refasten your knife to the end. You can use it to keep a Terry at bay until one of us can get it."

Did Joel just call those creatures Terries? What does that even mean? DeJuan looked at him and then at the rod, not so sure about its usefulness. Nevertheless, he reached for it, even though he wished it were a pistol, or better yet, a machine gun.

Then he heard a rapid clicking sound fade away. His heart, which had just started to slow, pumped hard again. "Did you hear that?"

"Sounded like it was running away," Robin whispered.

They listened for a minute, and then Joel waved them forward. They tiptoed past the mock bedrooms, then turned left, and continued past several more mock bedrooms. The showcases seemed to go on forever.

Joel suddenly shot up his arm and froze. Everyone else also stopped. After a few seconds Robin eased forward.

"What is it?" she whispered.

"The cabinet ahead. I heard a faint scratching sound from it," he whispered. He signaled for

DeJuan to go forward. "I need you to go over to the right side it and yank the door open. We'll be ready in front."

DeJuan wondered how much more excitement he could take. He mostly wondered why he needed to open the door though? Then he realized it made sense since he didn't have a real weapon, so he did as he was ordered. Besides, he would have the door to hide behind. The others would have to fight whatever was inside.

When he was in position, he glanced at Joel and Robin. They braced themselves in front of the cabinet, swords raised over their heads. Bill stood off to the other side with his spear pointed toward the cabinet.

Joel nodded to DeJuan. DeJuan pulled on the door, but it stuck. He grabbed the handle with two hands and yanked on it. Then he yanked harder. It suddenly popped open, and he almost tripped backwards over a chair. He stayed hidden behind the door though.

A loud shrieking scream pierced the quiet. DeJuan grabbed the handle again, and he pulled the door wide-open past him as Robin and Joel lowered their swords. Inside, a woman cowered. It explained the stuck door; she had desperately held it closed from the inside.

"No me hagas daño. ¡Por favor! ¡Por favor! ¿Esos monstruos han desaparecido? No dejes que me hagan daño." Her speech was so rapid, DeJuan had trouble following it.

"Do you speak English?" DeJuan asked.

"Si, yes."

"Come out. You are safe with us."

She burst out of the cabinet and threw her arms around DeJuan and put her head on his chest. "Estaba tan asustada. Tan asustado."

"What did she say," Robin asked.

"She said she was scared," DeJuan answered.

"You speak Spanish?" Robin asked.

DeJuan held up his hand, put his first finger close to his thumb. Just a little.

"Si, they tried get me. What those monstrous?" the woman asked.

"Dinosaurs," Robin answered.

"Dinosaurios? How's possible?" the woman asked.

"We will explain later. This is DeJuan, Joel, Bill, and I'm Robin."

"Camila!" She pounded a finger into her chest. "Camila Estavez Tormenta."

"Camila, let's get you out o' here," Robin said.

"Are there others?" Joel asked.

Camila shrugged. "Don't know if still here."

DeJuan was sort of sorry Camila no longer wrapped herself around him. She was soft and warm and smelled good enough to make him almost forget the danger around him. He glanced at her. She was short and thin with shoulder-length hair that curled toward the ends. Her skin was tanned, and her big brown eyes sparkled when she looked back at him.

Joel again took lead.

"Did …" Camila started to ask. Joel spun around fast and put a finger over his mouth.

They continued forward past the mock children's rooms and then ahead to the cafeteria.

"Anybody here?" Joel shouted and then listened carefully for any sound from survivors or more raptors. Nothing but dead silence.

Camila turned and looked at DeJuan with an expression that silently asked, "Why does he get to yell after he shushes me?" DeJuan smiled and shrugged. He would explain later.

They turned right and went down the stairs. They found kitchen utensils. They picked out several chef's knives with eight-inch blades and a large meat cleaver before they continued. They wound their way through the various sections without coming across anything else dangerous. They found some longer and stronger rods and stuck the tapered handles of the chef's knives into them. DeJuan would get one good jab with them before the blade would likely pull out of the rod. DeJuan sure hoped it wouldn't come to that. But on the other hand, it was a big blade; one jab could do a lot of damage.

They wound their way, for what seemed like an eternity to DeJuan, through the store until they came to a set of restrooms. Joel checked them out but found nothing to report.

After he returned, they turned left and took a few steps before they all froze. A series of dark red streaks stained the floor here too. They scanned around for more raptors. Then the lights flickered and went out.

Chapter 9 - DeJuan

O nly a very dim light remained. Camila gasped, and DeJuan was sure she was on the edge of panicking.

"Everything's okay, Camila." DeJuan didn't really believe it himself, but he wanted her to feel safe when she was near him.

"Wha … wha … what happened?" Camila asked.

"The fuel tank on the emergency generator just went dry," Robin whispered. She flicked on a flashlight as did Bill and Joel. They swept beams around them for a minute before Joel called them together.

Joel huddled them close. "Listen, the darkness in here seems scary. But believe me, we have the advantage here. From here on forward, there's no carpeting. If there are raptors moving around, we'll hear them. The clicking of their claws gives them away. If they do come at us, they will be blinded by our lights, and we can easily take them out. As we go forward, I will call out a few times to check for survivors." He paused and took a quick peek out ahead. "Otherwise, we're all to stay quiet so that we can hear their movements. I'll take lead. Bill, you watch the rear. Robin, cover our left flank, DeJuan, our right. Camila, you stay safe in the middle of all of us."

Joel took the lead without even asking if they were all good with the plan. He was in charge, and everyone knew it. He swept his beam back and forth and up the stacks. DeJuan guessed they would spot the reflection of the raptor's eyes if one were close. The others followed quietly as the light beams bounced around constantly. DeJuan wished he had a light too since he felt exposed on his side where it was dark. Far above them, scattered sky lights let light in, but not enough light to show what might be lurking on each side of them in the deep aisles, mostly hidden by dark shadows. The tall stacks of goods they passed seemed like mountains in the low light. Joel stopped.

"Wha... Why'd we stop," Robin asked. DeJuan realized she was as nervous as he.

"More bodies ahead," Joel whispered. They slowly stepped forward until they came upon the bodies.

Camila glanced down at what the flashlight beams revealed. She gasped and buried herself into DeJuan's arms.

DeJuan avoided looking down and instead searched for any sign of the raptors. With their kill on the floor, it didn't seem likely they were far away.

Joel reached down and checked for wallets in the pockets of the two dead men. No identification found. He picked up an ID tag from nearby on the floor and stuck it in his back pocket.

They resumed forward. The light level increased enough to where they saw their surroundings without the flashlights as they reached an area with large windows.

Joel reached into a bin he passed and tossed rolls of duct tape to DeJuan and Bill. Then he yelled out to see if anyone were around to answer his call. His voice echoed through the building, but there was no answer.

After the guys taped up the tips of their spears and made one for Camila, they tiptoed through the checkouts, wary of anything hidden behind the registers. On the other side was a food mart. Nearby, were more restrooms. Joel went inside each, and then, after he returned, he shouted around the room a few times. Again, there was only the echo of his voice for an answer.

Joel turned toward the rest of the group. "Well, if there were any more people here before, they're gone now or dead. Let's get out of here." He turned, led them through the exit doors and down the ramp to the lower level. They unlocked the east side door and stepped out into the hot mid-afternoon air. Between them and the mall, a raptor stood. However, it turned its tail to them and raced off toward the east.

"I think that was the last one we heard from upstairs," Joel said. "It's now learned to fear humans, at least if we are in a group and armed."

Bill said, "But other raptors don't know that."

"Yet," Joel added.

DeJuan turned to Robin and whispered, "Where's this guy from? He was like all Rambo in there."

"We don't really know." Her eyes fixated on Joel. "He only started at the mall about two months ago. We know he was in the military, but he hasn't talked about it. At least not yet. Bill and I think he was special ops. We're not even sure which branch he was in."

"Why's he a mall cop, then?" DeJuan asked. "No offense meant."

"None taken, sweetie. We think he suffered from PTSD. Post-traumatic stress disorder," Robin whispered.

"Yeah, I know what it is."

"Kay. Well, we think he got out because he saw something that got to him. Haunted him. Maybe still does. But that's just our little theory."

"Hypothesis, you mean," DeJuan corrected her.

Robin turned toward him, her faced scrunched up. "What?"

"Enough chatter back there. Let's move out," Joe ordered.

Chapter 10 - DeJuan

T he group crossed the open space to the mall without trouble. They were wary of any dinosaurs that might have sneaked into the mall as well, but they didn't spot any on their climb up the first two levels. They were climbing the last escalator up to the third level when the power suddenly went out. However, the mall's skylights still provided plenty of light in the middle courtyard and in the food courts.

"I guess the generator finally ran out of fuel," Bill said.

"Thanks, Captain Obvious." Robin smirked at him, but Bill ignored the comment. They reached the third level food court.

"Still plenty of light in the food court, and even the walkways," DeJuan said.

"Yeah, for now," Robin replied.

"Inside those stores, it's really dark though," Bill said.

DeJuan had smelled the burnt greasy odor of burgers, like a backyard barbeque, before they had even started up the first escalator. When they reached the southern food court, they saw electric grills had been set up. They grabbed clean foam plates and loaded them with burgers and bags of chips, and they snatched up cans of soda and bottles of water.

After DeJuan thanked the guy who had manned the grills, the guy said he wished he could have finished a few more burgers before the power had turned off. The five of them sat down at a table near where Alanna leaned against the railing. She came over and sat with them after she grabbed one of the bottles of water. Joel introduced her to Camila.

Alanna glanced at her. "She the only one there?"

"Only one alive, yeah." Joel nibbled at his burger.

Two men DeJuan didn't recognize sat at a table not far from them. "Who are the new guys?"

"They were on the highway like me when we got poofed here," Alanna replied.

The two young men stood up and stretched. Then they strutted over closer. DeJuan noticed they had left their empty plates, beer bottles and other garbage on the table. Both of them wore dark sweatpants and hoodies. A black man who seemed to be the leader had a head full of dreadlocks with an average build while the other, a white guy, appeared to have a shaven head and was a bit bigger and more broad-shouldered. A little hard to tell about the hair though because of the backwards inside-out baseball cap he wore.

"Saw ya lookin' my way," dreadlocks said.

"We're just wondering what's your story," Robin replied. "We'd not seen you before our little mission."

"Mission? Huh."

"Rescuing anybody that needed rescuing from over at Ikea."

"How 'bout dat," dreadlocks replied.

DeJuan noticed the man didn't ask if anyone had been rescued.

"Miss Dolencourt says you were on the highway behind her when we got zapped here," Robin said.

"Dat's right."

"You have a name?" Robin asked.

"What's yours, sugar?"

"Robin and you are?"

"Tones."

"Is that a first name or last?"

"It's da one ya can call me."

"I'm grabbin' another bottle," baseball cap said. He headed toward one of the counters.

"Grab two, Scar," Tones shouted. He turned and glanced at the swords which leaned against the table. He reached over and picked one up. He carefully ran his thumb over the blade. A drop of blood oozed to the surface of his thumb, and he smiled. He started walking away while still clutching the sword.

Robin clenched her fists. "Hey! Hey! Where the hell do you think you're going with that? That's mine."

"Was yours. But ya know—possession ..." He held up the sword, indicating he had just claimed it for his own.

Joel stood up and picked up his sword. "Unless you are looking for trouble, I suggest you hand it back to Robin."

DeJuan wondered if there was going to be a sword fight. An old-fashioned one like those from the movies, perhaps like the one from *The Princess Bride* or the one from *Pirates of the Caribbean*. He was betting on Joel.

Tones slowly turned around. "If ya wanna fight, it won't be dat kinda fight." He pulled his hand out of his hoody pocket, and it held a revolver. "Slide dat one over too. Scar could use one."

"Go to hell!" Joel said.

Tones waived the black barrel of the gun at him. "Ya gonna be stupid 'bout dis or what?"

"Joel, just give it to him," Robin said. "It's not worth your life."

"Be smart and listen to da bitch," Tones said.

Joel glared at Tones for a bit, glanced at Robin and the others and then tossed the sword at Tone's feet. DeJuan suspected Joel didn't do it out of fear for himself.

Scar appeared as he carried two beer bottles toward Tones. "Hey Jimmy, what's shakin'," he asked.

"Got a sword for ya."

Scar picked it up and admired it. "Cool, bro. Looks like one of those them ninjas use."

"I can't place your accent, but you're not from around here. Are you?" Joel asked.

Jimmy Tones smirked. "No need for ya ta know."

Joel glowered at them. "I was told you were driving on the highway when we got poofed here. Is that true?"

"Poofed?" Jimmy snickered.

"Is it true?" Joel asked again.

"Why ya wanna know?" Jimmy asked.

"A friend of ours was shot up on the parking ramp. Did you have anything to do with that? Can't help but notice you've got a gun."

Jimmy rolled his shoulders. "Mm. We were there."

"He's dead."

"Was business deal going down. We'd nuttin' ta do with da shooting. Dat's dem Chicago dudes. Everybod dare had guns, 'cept your friend. His m'stake."

"And where are the Chicago guys now?"

"Dead."

Joel raised an eyebrow. "Dead?"

"They drove over da ramps. Ask da pretty bitch." Jimmy pointed at Alanna. "She saw it go down." He turned and walked away with Scar.

DeJuan turned toward Alanna as did the others. "It's true," she said. "I tried to stop them, but only those two stopped. The others flew off the end of the ramp. I wanted to go see if they were still alive, but there was a big dinosaur down there tearing their cars apart. A rex, I think. I just got into my car and got the hell out of there at fast as I could after that."

"Those guys are trouble even if they didn't shoot Emilio," Robin said.

"What are we going to do with Emilio?" Bill asked.

"We should bury him," said Joel. "What do we use to dig the grave?"

"Get some shovels and pickaxes from Sears," Alanna replied.

"They don't have tools here at this Sears," Bill said.

"Yes, they do," Alanna replied. When the faces around the table suggested skepticism, she added, "Just before you came back, I was talking to Marge, I think that's her name. She was a custodian over there, and she said there was a big tool section down on the first floor. I know she mentioned shovels."

Robin turned and punched Bill in the arm. "You idiot!"

"Guys, guys, look down!" DeJuan shouted. "Now!"

"What the hell," Robin shouted. Below them on the first level three raptors raced about. They stopped, and their snouts went up into the air. "Great timing. They would show up right after those SOBs stole our damn swords."

"It's the food," Joel said. "They smelled the burgers and found their way in."

"I am beginning to really hate dinosaurs," Robin said.

The raptors seemed wired and constantly swiveled their heads. They looked up at where the cooked meat odor originated.

"It's only a matter of time before they find their way up here," Joel said.

"Damn! What do we do?" DeJuan asked. Unlike Robin, he was sure he hated dinosaurs.

"Raptors!" Joel yelled. "Everyone, get to Macy's. Now!"

Suddenly, DeJuan found himself in the midst of a stampede toward Macy's. He glanced over the edge as he ran with the others. He spotted another raptor in the central amusement park area. That made at least four of them.

"Bill, DeJuan, L'Troy, you three have to protect the rear of the crowd. Make sure everyone gets inside Macy's," Joel ordered. "Then pull the grill gate down. Get others to help."

On his way, DeJuan helped a man and then a woman who had each tripped or got knocked to the floor. After they reached Macy's, Joel went straight for the back toward the kitchen section as DeJuan, Bill and L'Troy rushed people inside. After the walkways appeared deserted, they lowered the grill gate and slammed it down against the mall floor.

Crashing and banging sounds echoed down the walkway from the direction of the food court. DeJuan wondered what Joel was doing in the back and wished Joel would reappear before the raptors appeared. Then he saw Joel march toward the gate carrying a chef's knife.

"Got everyone back there making more spears and guarding the escalators," Joel said.

They heard a distant scream of a woman.

"Damn!" Joel cursed. A few seconds later, two raptors and then a third trotted up the hall into view. DeJuan backed away, but Joel stayed put as he practically leaned up against the gate.

"Back up," DeJuan said. Joel seemed frozen, almost mesmerized by the raptor. "What are you doing? Are you crazy? Get away from the gate."

Joel continued to ignore him. What was he doing? He was acting all crazy again.

As the first raptor strutted up to the gate, it cocked its head back and forth and pivoted it around. DeJuan realized it eyed Joel. It gave a little chirp and then leaped straight at him.

Hind legs with sharp claws flew through the bars of the gate directly at Joel, but he dodged aside at the last split-second.

He grabbed one of the raptors front arms and pulled it tight against the gate. Feathers flew in the air. At the same time, he drove the large knife into the chest of the raptor, pulled it out and then stuck it in a second time before he let go of the creature's arm.

The raptor's body fell backwards, but it still hung backwards from the gate by its legs stuck through it. The second raptor meanwhile jumped at Joel, but Joel rolled back out of its reach before its death claws could reach him.

DeJuan recovered from his initial shock of Joel's actions and thrust his spear at the second raptor. The spear hit the gate and was deflected away from the middle of the belly where he had aimed. However, the blade sliced along the hip of the raptor. Blood dripped onto the floor.

The raptor pulled back and screeched as it raced back down the hall in the direction from which it had come. A trail of red spots dotted the walkway in its wake. The third raptor which had trailed behind the first two, turned to flight instead of attacking.

There was blood all over Joel's shirt. DeJuan at first assumed it was the raptor's blood, but there was a big rip in the shirt. Joel noticed DeJuan staring at it and looked down at his belly. He opened the front, ripping buttons off his shirt.

"You're bleeding," DeJuan said.

"It's nothing. Just a scratch. A band aid will hold it together," Joel said.

Alanna rushed over once she heard that Joel was hurt.

"It's nothing," Joel said. "He's just overreacting."

"Let me see it," she insisted. She pulled the shirt away from the wound for a quick peek before she gently laid it back over the wound. She ordered him to lay down. Then she pulled a jacket off a rack next to her, balled it up and put it under his head.

Freeda and another flight attendant ran up. "We can handle this. We've had first aid training," Freeda said.

"I've had training too," Alanna answered. "The wound doesn't look too bad. Mostly, just a surface scratch. But there is small puncture at the end of it." She peeled back the shirt to show them. "The bleeding has already mostly stopped, but it should be covered, so it doesn't start again. What I need are some cotton balls. You should be able to find them over by the cosmetics. And find some type of tape."

"I really don't need that. I'll be just fine," Joel said as he tried to sit. Alanna put a hand on his shoulder and gently pushed him back down.

"There will be time to play superhero later. Right now, just lay there and let us fix you up," she said.

Chapter 11 - Joel

After a couple of hours, a few people crept out of Macy's and other places of hiding and cautiously roamed the third level. Soon nearly everyone was out, but most kept a watchful eye on the lower levels. All the burgers were gone, and the electric grills had been smashed. Not that it mattered since they didn't have electric power anymore.

Bill, Robin, and a bandaged-up Joel went down the escalators and scouted out the lower levels. They confirmed all the raptors had disappeared from the mall, but two more people had been killed during the raptor raid.

Joel wondered what happened to Jimmy Tones and Scar. The pair had disappeared again, but he was sure the raptors hadn't gotten them. They were too evil to end like that. Besides, he would have expected remains of theirs such as clothing. Even if they were dragged away, the swords would have been left behind. No, they were holed away somewhere.

A couple of hours had passed since the raptor incident. Joel plopped down at a table with Bill, Robin and DeJuan in the south-side food court area after he had asked a couple of the night cleaning staff to stay stationed above the opening on the southeast corner to watch for any dinosaurs that approached the gaping hole again. Next time, they might have a warning if they were in danger.

Father O'Brien approached them. "I am hoping that I might be able to ask a favor from the four of you."

"What is it you need, Father?" Bill asked.

"I have gathered up the remains of the two recently departed up here, Anita Copa and Jackson Alistar. Our faith insists that we should bury their remains and give last rites for them, as well as for the man who suffered the heart attack, Kenneth Steindraught. I need somebody to dig the graves, and I am hoping I might get some volunteers."

"There can't be much left of those people," Robin said.

"Sadly, you're right," Father O'Brien replied. "In fact, in Kenneth's case, we don't have any remains. Nevertheless, we should bury what remains we have. In Kenneth's case, just some scraps of clothing. It is a sign of our faith that we believe they will be resurrected into the Kingdom of Heaven."

"Those are not the only dead, Father," Robin said. She told him about their friend, Emilio, and the remains they saw over at Ikea. Father O'Brien suggested they return to Ikea for the remains, unless they thought it too dangerous a trek. Then he moved on to speak to the people at the next table.

"Night's fast approaching," Bill said. "I don't think I want to be out after dark."

"Yeah, we need to hole up somewhere. Maybe Sears or Nordstrom for the night." Robin winked at Bill. "Maybe we could find a nice queen size bed we could snuggle up in."

Joel laughed to himself. Bill seemed to hate the mock flirtation and still had not figured out Robin did it because she liked him. Or maybe he didn't know where to go with their relationship, so he pretended not to understand.

"We'll make it through the night," DeJuan said. "What concerns me is not tomorrow. It's the day after that. And the one after that. And the one after that."

"Okay, but how long do you suppose we'll be stuck here?" Bill asked.

"Nobody knows. We should not count on getting poofed back." DeJuan snapped his fingers in the air when he said *poofed*. "Those people in and around Brown's Station disappeared back in March, and they still haven't been found."

"Crap!" Bill cussed. "I thought you would say something like that."

A man headed towards their table. Joel recognized him as one of the survivors from the plane. A little on the short side, with balding through the middle of the scalp, and a face that hadn't been shaved in a couple

94 : MJ Konkel

of days. A cheap suit covered a body shaped like a butternut squash with legs. The man weaved, obviously intoxicated.

"What kinda cops you have in this place?" The man wagged a finger at Joel, Bill, and Robin. "Couldn't protect us from the freaking dinosaurs. And now it's those damn thugs." He looked at Father O'Brien. "Sorry for my language." Then he turned his ire back on Joel, Bill, and Robin, forgetting about the priest. "You guys are freaking worthless. A disgrace to those uniforms."

Joel was about to ask the man what had happened that had upset him so much, but just then Camila flew out of nowhere onto the man's back. He crumpled to the floor from the impact and threw up his arms to cover himself as she sprawled on top of him and swung away at his head.

She yelled, "Cállate bastardo! Estas buenas personas nos están ayudando y todos ustedes maldicen ante ellos. Bastardo!"

DeJuan wrapped his arms around her hips and pulled her off the man. "It's all right, Camila. You don't have to wallop on him."

"He's suciedad," she shouted. "Suciedad!" She thrusted a finger at the man.

DeJuan held on to her until she calmed down enough for him to lead her to an adjacent table, although her eyes still threw daggers at the man. Bill and Robin helped the man to his feet until he pushed them away from him. Then he rubbed his cheek where one of Camila's long fingernails had scratched.

"Are you all right, Mister?" Bill asked.

"Mr. Thadius." He pointed a finger at Camila. "What the heck was she yelling at me?"

DeJuan smiled. "She said you need a bath. She's worried about your health." Joel doubted it was an accurate translation.

"Yeah, right! That woman's plain crazy." Mr. Thadius jabbed a finger in Camila's direction. "She should be thrown in jail too." He stared straight at Joel, seeming to think Joel was in charge. Camila snarled and looked like she was ready to pounce and start pounding on the man again, but DeJuan held her by her arm. He whispered into her ear, and she stomped away but obviously remained angry.

"I'll take it into advisement." Joel caught a heavy odor of alcohol from the man's breath. "You seem a bit calmer now. Maybe you can tell us what got you so worked up."

"I found a bottle of good tequila over at a joint called The Cantina ... ah ... something or other down there." He waved toward the walkway behind them. "I was just minding my own business in there when that n... young man with the funny hair came marching in." Joel was sure the man was about to utter a racist remark, but he probably noticed DeJuan stood off to the side listening. Probably worried DeJuan would pounce on him next. If he did, Joel was not about to pull him off the man. At least not right away.

Mr. Thadius leaned his hands on a table. "They told me to get the hell out of there, or they would 'pop a cap in my ass.' The smaller guy, he stuck a damn gun right in my face."

"And then what happened?" Joel asked.

"Well, I got the hell out of there. Was afraid I was going to get shot."

"That was the wise thing to do. But what do you expect us to do? Those guys have at least one gun. We do not have any." Joel waved empty hands in front of him.

"I don't know, but you're the cops. You figure it out. But something has to be done about them."

"If we figure out something, we will." Joe didn't add that it wouldn't necessarily be because of the man's reported incident.

"Ah … Maybe I just need to get some sleep. But I'll say it again. Those guys are a menace. You guys are the police here, right?"

"We'll add your grievance to the list against them," Robin said. "It's getting to be a pretty long list though."

"Damn thugs." Mr. Thadius yawned and rubbed his eyes with his thumbs. "Where can a guy get some rest and not have to worry about stinkin' dinosaurs?"

"Sears or Nordstrom's stores have been opened up. We'll close their gates for the night," Robin said.

"Any place that isn't so … so wide open? You know away from… others?"

Joel and Robin looked at each other. Robin spoke up. "Try the Lovesac. It's over on the west end on this level. It may or may not be still locked."

Mr. Thadius stumbled off in the direction she pointed him.

After Mr. Thadius was out of earshot, Joel asked, "Why did he assume I'm in charge?" He instinctively took charge when action was required, but he had no desire to be the police chief.

"You three are the police here," DeJuan replied. "You're wearing the uniforms."

"We're freaking mall security. Not police," Robin replied.

"If you don't want to be cops, take off the uniforms. There's a whole mall full of clothes to choose from."

"We can't just take stuff from the stores," Bill said. "After all, we're supposed to be the security here to stop that type of thing."

"This is a survival situation, isn't it?" DeJuan asked.

"Yeah, so?"

"I think he's trying to say the law says we can take what we need for survival under circumstances like this," Robin said.

"Actually, I was trying to say the law doesn't apply in this world. But I guess, it amounts to the same thing. By the way, which of you is really in charge?"

Joel laughed along with Robin.

Bill returned to the table with Camila. "None of us," he said. "We are all at the same level. George was in charge, but he's not here. I guess, technically, it now would be Robin since she's been here the longest. You know. Seniority."

"Oh, no!" Robin no longer laughed. "You're not going to pin a sheriff's badge on me. I'm not in charge here, and I'm leaving."

"Where are you going?" Bill asked.

"Out of here."

"But to where?" Bill asked.

"Back down to the security room to get the master keys," Robin answered. "I want to be able to open a store with gates for Mr. Thadius." And then after she took a few steps, she added, "And then lock it back up."

Joel laughed, pretty sure she was just kidding. Then he stopped laughing. Perhaps she was serious. Then he laughed harder. Mr. Thadius could go to Nordstroms instead if the Lovesac was locked. But then again, they should be able to open the other stores without breaking in as people had done at The Cantina Norte and a few other places.

"You got keys for everything here?" Camila had just returned.

"We have to be able to let firemen into any place there could be a fire. So, yes, we have keys for all the shops," Bill answered. He turned toward Robin. "Hey! Wait up! I am going with you. No one should go down there alone."

Robin stopped and turned. "Wow! How about that? Our very first date."

Bill rolled his eyes. Joel wondered how much more obvious Robin would have to get. Did Bill not like her, or was he gay?

Father O'Brien returned to the table where Joel sat. "I overheard the conversation over here."

"Oh, Father. Forgive me for I have sinned," Camila said.

"Relax. All is forgiven. I was ready to cold-cock the guy myself," Father O'Brien replied.

You, Father, seguramente no," Camila said.

"Yes, me. I have already asked for forgiveness for my thoughts. Anyway, I was passing by the Cantina when I heard that incident happening. It wasn't exactly as Mr. Thadius described it. He was getting loud in there, and those young men overheard him while passing by. They stepped in, and Mr. Thadius said some disparaging words, including the 'N' word. That is when they threatened to 'pop a cap.' They actually showed some restraint in not escalating it to further violence."

"Perhaps their restraint was due to your presence," Joel said.

"Perhaps," Father O'Brien replied. "But I'd rather believe there's at least some goodness in the hearts of those men."

"Perhaps, Father. But right now, I don't share your belief in them." Everyone had their own beliefs about the world and the people in it. It was apparent Father O'Brien believed in the general decency of people. Joel kept quiet about his beliefs, among them the evil he believed the two thugs were capable of. They were criminals, and he was certain they would continue to cause trouble.

Chapter 12 - DeJuan

DeJuan questioned his sanity. Why had he agreed to help retrieve the remains of the dead? Hadn't the last trip over given him nightmares all night?

He didn't believe in Father O'Brien's vision of the souls going to Heaven. Even if he did, he didn't see the need for the bodies anymore. So, why was he doing this? Maybe he was just following along, trying to be helpful. He really believed himself to be a good man.

Or maybe he wanted to be seen as a good man in the eyes of Camila who was a devout Catholic and believed in Father O'Brien's vision. His last thought gave him pause. He clearly felt an attraction for her and even a sense of protectiveness over her. But on the other hand, they were clearly very different people. Their personalities and their beliefs. Not to mention the situation they were in was hardly seemed ideal for starting something. He didn't even know what she thought about him. She clearly liked him. But was that all there was to her feelings? Was she even unattached?

"This time we have an actual plan," Joel said.

DeJuan ended his contemplation and looked around at the others. A plan at least gave him some measure of confidence. They had all survived their last adventure at Ikea without a plan, and they were better prepared this time. There were eight of them, a small army in comparison to the last outing. Robin and Bill had earphones and mics which allowed them to communicate with observers on top of the West Parking Ramp and what remained of the East Parking Ramp. In addition, their spears were improved. Joel had found some spare handles for shovels, and they attached knives with eight-inch blades via copper tubing to the ends. That provided them spears with much stronger shafts and much larger blades on their ends, and the blades were more securely attached.

Still the thought of purposely going back to where they had been attacked by raptorsaurs with their four-inch-long sickle claws struck him as a bit of lunacy. And he was a chest-deep in it. He couldn't turn back now, though, and make himself look the part of a coward.

Robin listened to the parking ramp spies over her earphone. "Hector and Alanna are saying the coast is clear. Little hand says it's time to rock and roll."

"Bahdi from *Point Break*," Bill said.

DeJuan glanced at them and wondered what that meant.

"We're going across in three groups. Bill and I will be first. Then you three." Joel pointed at DeJuan,

David and Freeda. "Robin, Carlos and An Dung, take up the rear. Any questions before we start?"

"Just one. We aren't hunting them again, are we?" Robin asked. "I mean not that it wasn't fun last time."

Joel laughed. "No, our mission is to go in, bundle the remains in cloth and retreat."

"So, no engaging the enemy, unless engaged upon," Robin said. "Got it."

Joel laughed and nodded while Freeda and David stared at them with their mouths open, probably wondering if it was too late to turn back. DeJuan smiled at Freeda and David to settle their nerves. He glanced back at Joel. Most times, he seemed like a normal dude, and DeJuan decided he liked him. But there were times the man just plain terrified him with his covert military style. Nevertheless, he had already come to trust Joel's leadership when it came to situations like the one they faced.

Joel and Bill marched across. After they paused for a minute and spied ahead from the line of trees on the corner opposite the intersection, they continued toward the Ikea building while DeJuan's group headed for the same trees. Once they reached the trees, DeJuan almost waved toward the top of the West Parking Ramp. He knew Camila was up there with Alanna and a couple of others, but then he thought better of it. It probably wasn't appropriate, so he merely stared in the direction for a few seconds before his group followed Joel and Bill toward the Ikea building. He hoped Camila was staring back.

Soon the whole party stood outside of the entrance to the building. They ducked inside single file through the same broken glass opening as before, starting with Joel who immediately climbed the escalator ramp which led to where the checkout section was located. Bright light streamed in through the windows near the exit, but the light level dropped off rapidly behind the registers far back into the huge room. Everyone had flashlights this time and quickly switched them on as they pushed forward. Penetrating beams danced every which way.

A clattering sound reverberated from deeper back in the building. Eight beams converged on where the noise originated. A flowerpot rolled in an arc across the floor, illuminated by several light beams. Rapid clicking noises echoed from farther back, and multiple beams shot out deeper into the room.

"What was that?" The man next to DeJuan held his spear out in a tight grip in the hand opposite of his light. The man was the custodian that had let them into Macy's the previous day. DeJuan had learned the man's name was Carlos Espadachin.

"Raptors," DeJuan replied. "But they were running away."

"Si, raptors," Carlos said. His light danced around in search of them, but DeJuan noticed the beam jittered. He couldn't blame the man for being scared.

Joel slowly advanced forward, stopped, and then knelt. His flashlight shone on a dark stain on the floor.

"This is where we saw two of the bodies yesterday," Bill explained to the others.

"But all that's left now is some blood on the floor." Joel stood up and pointed his flashlight beam ahead in a slow sweep across the room. "Everyone, back up."

Once they were back past the checkout, Joel led them left down past a deli shop and toward the escalator which led to the second floor.

Suddenly a whooshing noise filled the hallway, and a bird flew over their heads. DeJuan ducked into a crouch as did everyone except for Joel.

Joel spun around and stared at all of them. "It was just a pigeon, for Christ's sake." He turned back toward the escalator and shook his head.

"Well, it scared the crap out of me," Bill said. "Just a figure of speech, Robin." He didn't leave Robin even a gap for one of her usual snide comments.

"Wait a minute," Robin said. Everyone halted. "I'm getting a message from Alanna. Alanna, can you repeat that?" She listened for a few seconds. "She says there's a herd of dinos moving toward this building."

"What kind?" Joel asked.

"She doesn't know, but thinks that they're not meat eaters," Bill answered. He also had an earphone and was closer to Joel.

"All right, then let's not worry about them for now and go forward. Single file up the escalator. Robin, go last and keep an eye on our rear."

Robin gave him a two-finger salute that, although seemingly sarcastic, somehow came off as respectful.

At the top, Joel stopped with DeJuan and the others close behind. There was light to the left of them toward the cafeteria where there were walls of windows but not in other areas. Plenty of dark places from which hidden raptors could hide and ambush them. The troop searched every nook and cranny their lights could reach before they continued forward toward where they had seen the other body.

The body was still there. It was even more gruesome than the last time. Much more flesh on the front side was torn away, and it already smelled bad.

DeJuan had to turn away. He instead scanned around the interior for any raptors. Joel and Bill spread out a blanket on the floor and then a plastic sheet over that. Next, they moved the body up over onto the plastic while the others stood guard. DeJuan knew from how Bill had vomited the last time, it had to be hard for him. He found a new respect for Bill. The guy showed he could reach down for extra when he needed it. Carlos and Freeda, on the other hand, each looked like they were going to take turns emptying their stomachs.

Joel and Bill quickly got the body wrapped and added some straps around it, so it wouldn't unwrap while they carried it. It didn't seem quite so bad once the body was all covered with the wrappings, and they wouldn't have to stare at the bloody remains. It didn't smell quite as bad either, though there still was an odor.

After they handed their spears to others, Joel and Bill grabbed the head and foot ends and carried the body down the escalator. They continued down the next escalator to the lower level, along with the rest of the group. They set the body down, and Joel and Bill took back their spears.

"I am going to scout out these new dinosaurs. Robin, you're with me. Everyone else stay put for now. Stay alert though and always watch your backside," Joel said.

"I'm coming too," DeJuan said. Joel gave him a stare that said to stay put, but DeJuan wasn't about to be deterred. "I'm pretty sure I know more about the different species of dinosaurs here than anyone else, which ones are dangerous, and which are not."

"Okay. But stay behind us and stay quiet."

"Showing off for your new girlfriend?" Robin teased.

DeJuan blushed. Camila wasn't his girlfriend, although he was very fond of her. But she wasn't the reason he felt the need to come with them.

They stepped out through the opening and slunk along the wall to the other side of the entrance. There, out in the ditches which lined Lindau, a dozen duck bill dinosaurs grazed. Red and orange crests on the tops of their heads like a tubular horn contrasted the dull gray of their bodies. The animals probably weighed between one to two tons each and ambled along on all four legs, although the back legs were much longer than the front legs. They slowly moved farther eastward as they munched on the shrubbery along the way and had just passed the intersection to the main entrance.

"*Hodiernusaurolophus*," DeJuan whispered. He stared in fascination of their appearance and behavior. These wouldn't bother them.

"What?" Robin asked.

"It's the scientific name given to this species. It means modern lizard crest. They were found in large numbers down around the Brown's Station Zone."

"Is there an easier name for them?" Robin asked. "Like something I can pronounce."

"You can call them hadrosaurs or duck bills. They are herbivores, very gentle and easily spooked."

"Then we don't need to worry about them?" Joel asked.

"No," DeJuan replied.

"Let's get across then," Joel said, "Have the rest of the troop catch up."

"Bill," Robin mumbled into her mic. "Have two people pick up the body and move out. These dinos won't bother us."

Two minutes later they were a company crossing toward the mall. They reached the line of trees on the northwest corner of the intersection. David and An Dung set the body down as they took a short rest. DeJuan stared at the duck bills. He had seen many pictures of them but had never seen live ones before. Pictures never do justice to the real thing. The dinosaurs had moved fifty yards further down from where they first saw them, and Joel signaled for everyone to move out again. David and An Dung picked the body back up, and they all marched out into the intersection.

Suddenly, two of the duck bills lifted their heads into the air, swung them around, and stared in their direction. They made bellowing noises, and the small herd took off as the animals rose onto their hind legs and sprinted away like ostriches.

"You're right about them being easily spooked," Robin said.

"It's not us that spooked them," Joel shouted. "Look!" He pointed in the opposite direction from the duck bills. A rex strutted toward them.

DeJuan remembered Joel had said to everyone to always watch their backside. He would have to remember that in the future and make it a habit. Assuming he survived long enough to have a future.

"Run!" Bill and Robin shouted. DeJuan and everyone else, except for Joel, took off for the mall. DeJuan glanced back at Joel who stared back at the Ikea building. That is where they should have gone since it was closer, but it was too late now. They had committed to the dash to the mall.

DeJuan glanced at the rex. It had picked up speed. DeJuan remembered he had read the rex had a top speed of about 25 mph, but the bigger they were, the slower they moved. Based on their distance, the rex's distance, and the fact that it was a monstrous rex, they would probably reach the mall doors before the rex. But would it stop or just smash through the glass doors?

He glanced over his shoulders and saw Joel had thrown his spear down and now ran too. David and An Dung carried the body and had fallen behind the rest of them. DeJuan looked over his shoulder as he ran. As Joel caught up to David and An Dung, he yanked the body away from them, and it tumbled to the road.

"Run!" Joel yelled. The three of them sprinted toward the door, but the rex was not far behind. It didn't seem likely all three would make it. An Dung was farthest behind, and DeJuan feared for him.

DeJuan stopped at the mall door and held it open while Joel sprinted through. DeJuan vigorously waved the others to hurry to the door. Not that they really needed extra motivation.

Surprisingly, the rex slowed down instead of chasing after An Dung and David. DeJuan watched as the rex approached the abandoned wrapped body, then picked it up by one end and gave a violent jerk of its head. The body twirled fifteen feet above the head of the rex before it crashed back to the ground with a thunk.

David and An Dung flew past DeJuan into the mall as he watched the rex fling the body yet again up into the air. This time the body came out of the wrappings and rolled across the pavement.

DeJuan turned away. No desire to watch the rex gulp down the body. He had been awakened by enough nightmares the previous night and did not need more fodder for the nightmares. He felt deeply disappointed they had come back with nothing to show for their troubles, and he was angry about the foolish risk they had just taken.

Ahead of him, Joel stopped, put his hands on his hips, and tried to catch his breath. He pointed back at the rex. "Will you look at that?"

DeJuan refused. Just the thought of it made his stomach turn. "I'm not watching another human body being devoured if I can help it."

"It's not eating the body."

"What?" DeJuan twisted his head around. The rex carried the body, draped across his jaw, away toward the west. "What's it doing?"

"Maybe he isn't hungry and is saving it for later."

"Maybe. But if he wasn't hungry why was he even out hunting? Doesn't make any sense."

"A lot doesn't make sense out here," Joel said. He scratched his belly.

DeJuan turned and pointed at Joel's mid-section. "How's the wound?"

Joel lifted the front of the t-shirt he wore and examined the wound. A little dried-up blood had seeped around the bandage, but, otherwise, it looked all right. He scratched around the taped-up wound. "It itches, but I'll live another day."

"I sure hope so. I hope we all do." DeJuan chuckled to himself. "You know, when I first came flying out here, I was supposed to go down to the Brown's Station Zone. I'd hoped to get a glimpse of a few of the dinosaurs while I was there." He chuckled again. "You know what they say about being careful about what you wish for. Because now I'd be perfectly happy if I never saw another freaking dinosaur the rest of my life."

"Amen to that, brother. Amen to that."

DeJuan softened in the presence of Camila's smile, and his anger dissipated. Besides, he thought, no one really got hurt. It really was just another adventure. One that someday he could tell his kids. If he ever had kids. If he lived long enough to have kids. If Camila or someone else would have him. The ifs were really starting to pile up.

Chapter 13 - Robin

In the afternoon they had a short funeral for all who had died since the poofing (which they had started calling the event of the previous morning). One moment they were in their world. Then poof; they were in the dinosaur world.

Robin and the others from the Ikea trip did not dig any of the graves. Father O'Brien said they had done enough and found a couple of other volunteers instead. Robin thought the priest might have felt some pangs of guilt for having asked them to put themselves in danger.

They buried Emilio and the few remains they had of the other dead. Father O'Brien spoke some prayers for them and the others who had perished, including the airplane pilots and the man taken at the lake by the monster. The priest said a few final words of comfort. Then most people wandered up to the third level food court on the north side to gather for a repass. Bowls of crackers, chips and salsa and vegetables were set out, and people mingled around.

Robin, Joel, Father O'Brien and DeJuan stood in a circle.

"Remember when Emilio sent the messages from the future through the copy machine?" Bill asked.

"Messages from the future?" Father O'Brien had a puzzled grin. "You must have a really high-tech copy machine down in that office of yours."

"Oh, don't tell that story," Robin begged.

Bill ignored her request. "Emilio sent Robin messages to the copy machine that were to Robin and signed by Robin From Your Future."

"Wait. How could she not know it was from one of you?" DeJuan asked.

"There is only one computer in the security center, so Robin assumed it had to come from that computer. None of us knew Emilio had put the password to the printer on his phone, so he was sending the messages from his phone. To continue the story: the first one he sent said Emilio was going to shout at her that night, but she should just ignore it because of bad news he had gotten earlier in the day.

"Well, Emilio yelled at her for some bogus reason which I don't even remember anymore, but Robin, big surprise, kept her cool that night. If you know Robin, you'd know how hard it must have been for her. Anyway, he went away and came back and apologized to her about ten minutes later. That set it up so she would believe the later messages."

"Come on! I did not really believe them," Robin protested. No one seemed to listen to her though.

"The next few messages were pretty plain. He would send one every few nights. Then he sent one that said a disaster was coming that couldn't be explained in a message, but she needed to stockpile toilet paper near her desk. Lots of it. When George, our supervisor, came in and asked why she had so much TP all around her desk, and if she were having problems, Emilio couldn't help himself. He was doing everything he could to stop himself from busting a gut."

Robin searched around the courtyard as Bill told the story. She needed an excuse, any excuse, to escape.

Across the food court, Jack Wanderluch poured charcoal briquettes into a grill he had found somewhere, possible at The Backyard Store. His wife and a few others sat at a food court table near him. He tossed a match into the pile of briquettes. Next to him a stack of raw steaks waited to be tossed onto the grill.

Joel tore away from the group and yelled at Jack to stop. Robin, as well as several others, followed. It was her big break to escape. She would have to figure out later how to get back at Bill for his treasonous act.

Jack put his hands on his hips and stared at Joel running toward him. "We're grilling enough of these for everyone who wants one. There're not just for us," he yelled.

Joel reached the man and stood in front of him, crossing his arms. "Don't care who they're for. You can't grill anything in here. It's gonna attract more raptors and rexes into the mall. That's what drew them in yesterday." The odors of the cooking burgers.

"Didn't I say to not cook them?" June, Jack's wife, said.

"You said they'd make us sick. But there's nothing wrong with these steaks. They're just barely thawed out." Jack shrugged his shoulders and waved his arms. "You said nothin' about dinosaurs smelling the meat." Jack replied.

"That's quite a nice necklace you have there, Mrs. Wanderluch," Robin said. She had noticed what appeared to be a large emerald necklace surrounded with rows of brilliant diamonds around the woman's neck.

"Oh, it's just something I've had for years. Fake stones, but they're pretty," Mrs. Wanderluch replied. She hid her hands behind her back.

Robin noticed the large diamond rings on each of Mrs. Wanderluch's hands before they disappeared. Robin frowned at her but didn't comment. It was bound to happen, and there was nothing they could really do about it. It probably didn't even really matter. Nevertheless, it further colored her opinion of the woman.

"But there's so much good meat in all the restaurants that's going to just spoil if it isn't cooked," Ron Sevendells replied. He, another of the plane's survivors, was the one who had happened to have found the steaks.

"We have to eat," Jack said.

"I can already smell some of it starting to go bad in the restaurants," Bill said. "Fishy smelling."

"I'll bet rotting meat draws them into the mall just as fast as cooking it," DeJuan said. "Maybe faster."

"Yeah, I was just having the same thought," Joel said.

"We definitely have to get rid of it," Robin said.

"Agreed," said Joel. He rubbed his forehead with the palm of his hand.

"What's wrong?" Robin asked.

"Nothing. Just a bad headache," Joel replied. "I'm going to go lie down somewhere for a while. Get some rest."

"So, are we all agreed then the meat and fish starting to get ripe has to leave the mall?" Robin asked.

"What about these steaks?" Jack asked. "It would be such a shame to throw them out. Filet mignon."

"Nobody wants to have to hide from those raptors again, but we do have to eat," Ron said.

"I've an idea," Bill said.

"Hey! All by yourself. That a boy." Robin clapped.

"Oh, you're just mad because of that story. Anyway, I was thinking about how half of the parking ramp on that side is gone." Bill pointed toward the eastern ramp.

"Now, nothing can come up because it is the ramp part on the outside edge that is gone," Robin said.

"Yeah, and we could use the walkway from the third level here over to the garage, and you could grill over there. But don't go too far out because the whole ramp structure may not be stable."

"Only one problem," Robin said. "There are stairs to get up the garage levels."

"I forgot about those. But there are only two on each level, right?" Bill asked.

"I think that's all that's left. We could just put a couple of guards above each of those stairwells," Robin said. "Only raptors could get up those anyway."

"Is there a way to block them off?" DeJuan asked. "I know we didn't try in the mall here because there are so many escalators, it just wasn't feasible. But if we need to block off only two stairways, maybe it would be."

Bill scratched his head. "I don't know."

"Maybe, we just have to make it difficult, painful even, to go up the stairs. Suppose we covered the stairs with several boxes worth of roofing nails," Robin said. "I'm pretty sure they would have those down in the tools section of Sears."

"I like that idea," Bill said.

"Maybe we can make them even more painful by pouring some battery acid over them so that stepping on them would be like getting stung by fire ants," Robin said.

"It would sure make stepping on them burn," DeJuan replied, "but the acid would corrode the nails away fast.

"What if I wet the nails down by spraying them with my mace?" Robin asked.

"Mm… I have some doubts about mace working against dinosaurs," DeJuan replied.

"A little bit can put down the biggest man. Gert him crying, and I've seen it work on dogs too," Robin said. She hated the way DeJuan shot down all her ideas.

"Yeah, people and dogs are mammals. But dinosaurs are closer to birds. You see capsaicin works on a GPCR, called the vanilloid receptor type one. The receptor has a different form in mammals than in birds."

"GCPR?" Robin asked. She couldn't be the only one who didn't know what the hell he just said.

"G-protein coupled receptor. The capsaicin will bind to those receptors in us, but it doesn't bind to the bird version of the receptor. Fascinating, isn't it?"

"It's weird." Robin had actually meant his fascination was the weird part.

"Not really. It's evolution. Capsaicin is the chemical in peppers that make them hot. Pepper seeds aren't digested by birds so when they eat the peppers, the seeds get dropped in their feces and that spreads the seeds around. Mammals, on the other hand, digest the seeds. By making a substance that burns on mammal tongues but has no effect on birds, it increases the chance birds instead of mammals will ingest the seeds and spread them. And you want to know what the weird part of this is?"

"Weird, all right." Robin decided she needed to learn how stop encouraging DeJuan.

"The weird part is that one mammal, us humans, developed a liking for that hot flavor and then, because we developed cultivation, spread the plants and diversified them far more than if pepper plants relied only on birds. I'd even guess if we'd never developed a taste for them, we'd be trying to eradicate pepper plants as just weeds."

"You're a wealth of knowledge. Just full of it. What does this have to do with mace?" Robin asked.

"I'm sorry. I got into my teaching mode. Capsaicin is the main ingredient in pepper spray. While mace originally was a solution containing cyanide, today's versions usually are only pepper spray."

"What do you suggest then?" Robin asked. "Maybe, I should just pee over them."

"Mm, that might work. It might also attract them. I have an idea, but I hate to suggest it because I have been campaigning against it for years, but tobacco smoke may be a good deterrent. Birds are very sensitive to people smoking around them. Maybe, we should ask smokers to volunteer as the guards. Have them light up a cigarette or better yet a cigar," DeJuan said. "I am not saying it will work for sure in keeping them away. But it might help. And I doubt it will attract them."

"How the hell do you know all this shit," Robin asked.

"I read a lot." DeJuan shrugged his shoulders. "And I remember almost everything I read."

"Nice story, Professor. But what the hell should we do with these steaks?" Jack asked.

"Close off this grill and let it cool," Robin said. "Grab another, or better, two of them grills and some more charcoal. And we'll set it up out on what's left of the ramp."

"I'll go find some roofing nails and boards," DeJuan said. "Can't forget a hammer."

"I'll go find some other people to volunteer as guards," Bill said. "Guards get the first steaks, right?"

Annoying as the Wanderluchs were, Jack was a master griller. Robin sat with Bill, DeJuan, and Camila as they enjoyed a meal of juicy grilled tender sirloin, grilled vegetables, and a bottle of Cabernet Sauvignon. They had arranged tables and chairs gathered from one of the restaurants onto the skyway that connected the mall to the parking ramp. Four other tables had people who dined at them and more tables were on their way. With closed doors on the mall side and windows all around, it seemed a safer dining spot than the food court since they didn't have to constantly worry about whether a pack of raptors was sneaking up the escalators. It didn't have much ambiance, and the view was mostly of the sides of the mall and the parking ramp. However, the windows also provided a partial view of a distant landscape and the sky.

"Look what the cat dragged in," Bill moaned.

"Yeah, well, I wish that cat would drag them back out." Robin frowned. "Or better, tear them to shreds."

DeJuan and Camila glanced toward the mall doors. Jimmy Tones and his sidekick had just stepped through the door. As they crossed toward the parking ramp, everyone watched but took care not to make eye contact.

The two strutted right up to the front of the line. Past people already waiting. Everyone quickly jumped out of their way and gave the two room to go wherever they pleased. The two stabbed with their forks a couple of steaks that had just come off the grill and plopped them onto plates.

They carried their plates and stood in front of the first arranged table, staring down at the people who sat around it. After a moment's hesitation, the people at the table picked up their plates and scrambled away. They settled on the floor down on the other end of the skyway. They left a bottle of wine behind which Jimmy picked up and sniffed. He took a swig and passed the bottle to Scar. The two set the swords on the table in front of them and sat down with their backs against the wall as the two cut into the steaks.

Bill muttered quietly enough not to be overheard beyond their table. "God, I hate those assholes."

Robin nodded in agreement. She was sure she hated them at least as much as he did.

Alanna came through one of the doors from the mall side. "There you are."

"Is something wrong?" Robin noticed worry lines on Alanna's face. Everyone else nearby turned toward Alanna too.

"It's Joel. I went to check on him. He was moaning, so I felt his head, and it's not just warm. He's burning."

Everyone scrambled from the table, and Alanna led the way as they left the remainder of their meal and hurried to where Joel lay. A few others from nearby tables followed as well.

A small crowd gathered around Joel. Camila had left to fetch a bucket of water and some cloths that could be soaked and used to blot him. Two others were sent out to find a thermometer, aspirin, and water to drink. Robin knelt over Joel and pulled up his shirt. She put her hand on his belly. It was on fire. She carefully peeled back the tape, but it took some of his skin with it. "Who thought duct tape on skin was such a good idea?"

"It was the only tape I could find at the time," DeJuan replied. "You know for 1001 uses now."

"He's not all to blame. I was the one who actually put it on," Alanna said.

Robin pulled away the cotton balls. The wound oozed yellow fluid, and it was very red around the area. "He's definitely got some type of infection. I know we couldn't find any antibiotic cream over at Macy's, but we should have at least redone the dressing since then."

"Agreed, but what do we do for him now?" Alanna asked. The contours of her lips and eyes were creased.

"We keep him as cool as we can. You know 'starve a fever.' Get some aspirin and make sure he stays well hydrated," Robin said.

"He really needs antibiotics," DeJuan said.

"No shit, Sherlock. But there's no pharmacy in the mall or Ikea. Our first aid kits don't include penicillin. Now, unless you can magically pull some out of your butt ..." Robin pulled a hand down over her face as if she could wipe away what she just said. "I'm sorry. I shouldn't have snapped at you."

"It's okay," DeJuan said. "I have a bottle of amoxicillin."

"You do?" Robin perked up. "That's great. Where is it?"

DeJuan took a deep breath before he answered. "It's in my backpack."

"Great! Well, go get it!" She wondered why he hadn't moved.

"Well ... umm."

"What's the problem?"

DeJuan shrugged his shoulders. "It's still on the plane,"

"Well ... Shit!" Robin cursed. That meant going through the woods that was home to the juvenile rex and who knew what other carnivores. Everyone from the plane spoke about a gigantic croc next to the plane.

"I'll go," Father O'Brien said. When DeJuan and Robin looked at him, he shrugged. "He is one of our flock. I don't believe the good Lord intends to take him from us at this time. It is my belief that this is merely a test of our determination and our resolve."

"Thanks, Father. I'm going too," Robin said. There was no way she was not going to do whatever she could for Joel.

"Me too," Bill added.

"I have to go," DeJuan said. "It's my bag."

After word spread about the expedition back to the plane, three more volunteered as well.

Chapter 14 - DeJuan

J oel still ran a high fever the following morning. The volunteers waited until light to get started. Bill tramped down the long grass in front of him as he marched. "I must be crazy."

"Plenty of evidence for that," Robin replied.

"Third time in three days I'm going out and putting myself in harm's way by my own choice," Bill said.

"Preaching to the choir, sister," Robin said. "But it's a lot of fun. Isn't it?"

"If either of you want to turn back, just say so," DeJuan said.

"No way," Bill said. "This is for Joel."

"Just saying, this is dangerous," Robin said. "Not saying I'm backing out. Like I said, fun."

They reached the end of the open grassland beyond the mall and started to enter the woodland to the south. DeJuan wasn't sure which was worse. In the open, he had felt exposed. If a rex had appeared out there while they were halfway to the wooded area, they would not have been able to outrun it. Robin joked she would only have to outrun Bill, not the rex. Bill didn't seem to think it was so funny.

In the woods, the trees could be used for cover, for dodging around and slowing the rex down. But the woods could hide raptors, small rexes, or who knew what else almost anywhere, just waiting to ambush a band of hikers. DeJuan thought about the one that had attacked them on the first day and how it had stalked them. That one was still out there somewhere, and the thought of it lurking in the woods gave him goosebumps.

Bill and Carlos took the lead; Robin and DeJuan watched the rear behind them as David, An Dung, and Father O'Brien were in the middle. At first, they progressed painfully slow as they tramped through thick low tangles of brush which scratched and clawed at them, but then their pace quickened once they came upon a trail heading in the same direction as theirs toward the plane.

Suddenly Bill and Carlos froze, causing the train to stop. Robin slowly eased forward to the front, and DeJuan followed her, but he still constantly glanced over his shoulder.

"Why'd we stop?" Robin whispered. "Oh!" Just ahead of them where the trail started into its next bend was a carcass.

"Appears to be a *Hodiernusaurolophus*," DeJuan whispered.

Robin stared at him.

"A duckbill." DeJuan rolled his eyes.

"It's not smelling that bad, at least from here," Bill said. "I don't think it's been dead that long."

"I don't like it here," An Dung whispered.

"Me either," Father O'Brien added.

"This is a game trail," Robin whispered. "We need to get off it and out of here. Whatever killed that will no doubt be back to finish it."

"The odor of the bloody flesh might be drawing in scavengers too," whispered DeJuan. "Like a big rex."

"Let's not talk about it and just get going," Robin whispered.

They turned left turn off the path, away from the ominous carcass, and into thicker woods. They had two advantages they didn't have the day they had escaped from the plane. First, they had better weapons with their spears rather than the flimsy stick DeJuan had tried to wield. Second, Bill had a compass in his possession, so they knew which direction was south in even in the thickest of the woods.

No one said a word during the rest of the trek through the woods. At one point DeJuan thought he heard branches crack behind them in the woods, but he couldn't judge the distance. He couldn't see anything back there. But as he had already quickly learned, not seeing something didn't mean it wasn't there.

Whenever anyone stepped on and snapped a stick, everyone froze for a short time and then gave the offender the eye before continuing as a reminder to watch where they stepped. This happened several times, but, with the ground littered with leaves everywhere, it was not always possible to spot a stick before it was stepped on.

They reached the bank which led down to the river and the lake and stopped to consider their route. Bill wanted to go down to the shore and follow it to where the plane was located. They quickly decided to follow the edge of the bank after DeJuan reminded them of the incident with the huge crocodile. They didn't have to straddle the bank's edge for long before the plane sat right in front of them.

Bill and Carlos led as they stepped over the edge on a path down the slope. DeJuan thought he heard a noise in the brush behind him but didn't spot anything. Then he almost ran into An Dung. Everyone had halted after only a few steps.

DeJuan stared down toward the plane. Next to wing closest to shore, a huge dinosaur waded in the lake. It was an equal in size to the rex that had been patrolling around the mall, but this was a very different type of dinosaur with a huge striking sail on its back. The sail was bell-shaped and extended from the base of its neck to the base of its tail. It had a longer, more narrow snout full of sharp-tipped teeth, and it had shorter hind legs than the rex. And its front limbs, although not as big as its back legs, were not the tiny arms of the rex. This gray-green monster stood in a few feet of water and faced parallel to the shore. Its head almost touched the wing of the plane they had to climb upon while its open snout was suspended close to the water.

"And what do you call this one?" whispered Father O'Brien at DeJuan.

"I don't know," DeJuan replied. "None of these were found in the Brown's Station Zone. Perhaps they are seasonal. It appears to be from the Spinosauridae family, but there's no scientific name for this species."

"I'm calling it a sailback then," Robin whispered.

"Not a scientific name, but sure. Works." DeJuan whispered.

"What do we do now?" Father O'Brien asked.

DeJuan stared down at the monster. "We wait. What else can we do?"

"Someone could lure it away," David said.

"Be bait for it you mean? You know how it always ends for the bait. I'm not volunteering for that," Robin said. No one else volunteered either.

The snout of the sailback suddenly plunged into the lake just below the wing of the plane. Whatever was in the sailback's snout was big and thrashed wildly about which threw huge sprays of water onto the wing of the plane. The sailback continued to clamp down despite all the wild thrashing and then it shifted its legs around as its victim continued to struggle. The dinosaur swung its long snout around and started to drag a body out of the murky lake. The sailback had locked its jaws around the jaws of a huge crocodile, maybe the same one that had killed the man earlier. The crocodile certainly looked big enough to be the same one. It couldn't fight back with its jaws clamped shut, nor could it use its tail to try to drag itself and the sailback into deeper water because they faced toward the shoreline.

The sailback hefted the crocodile, still locked in its jaws, up until only half of the croc was on the ground and then dragged it up the slope. The croc continued to whip its powerful tail around but only scattered sand and dirt with it. DeJuan was amazed by the strength of the dinosaur. The crocodile looked like it had to weigh a thousand pounds, but it was hard to judge when it was held by such a monster of a dinosaur.

DeJuan was so mesmerized by the sailback he almost didn't hear Robin whispering for everyone to get off the path and hide. He scrambled sideways along the bank and scooted under some bushes along the upper part of the bank.

He flipped over onto his belly and peered upward. A minute later the twitching tail of the crocodile passed up and over the bank, closely followed by the sailback's front and then back legs. He noticed the underbelly of the dinosaur was a dirty white or light gray color in contrast to the rest of it. He also just realized it wasn't a crocodile it had caught. The sailback was too tall for DeJuan to see its upper body from under the bush, but he got a good glimpse of what it dragged.

After he no longer heard the alligator's tail being dragged along, he eased himself toward the trail the sailback had used to climb up the bank. The others had come out by then too. DeJuan crawled up to the edge of the bank and peeked over the top.

"Is it still going away?" Bill asked.

"It's about fifty yards off and still going up the trail," DeJuan whispered.

Father O'Brien crawled up next to DeJuan to get a view of the beast for himself. "Why do you think it's dragging that croc away so far?"

"Maybe it's taking it back to feed the young uns," Robin answered. She crawled up immediately after the priest.

"That was an alligator, not a crocodile," DeJuan said.

"Crocodile, alligator. How can you tell the difference?" Robin asked. "Oh, I know. Because we would have seen it after a while."

"What?" asked Bill.

"We saw it later, so it must have been a gator." Everyone groaned.

DeJuan ignored the joke and jumped into his explanation. "An alligator has a rounded U–shaped snout, while a crocodile has narrower V-shaped snout. Also, the alligator has an overbite while a crocodile does not."

"And what does the diff mean for us mortals?" Robin asked.

DeJuan shrugged his shoulders. "Probably not much. Other than alligators tend to be less aggressive than crocodiles." Not that it did any good for that man who was pulled under on the first day. "Also, I don't know if that'll be true of the alligators here." He craned his neck back toward the plane. "I should go get my pack before that monster decides to come back."

"A couple of us should stay here and watch, just in case it does," David said. "I'll stay." Carlos raised his finger and pointed at himself as he volunteered as well.

DeJuan now led as he and four others climbed down the slope toward the plane. Across the lake, he spotted two more large sailbacks. It appeared those two stood in a swampy strip that separated the lake from the river. Those dinosaurs didn't worry him though.

"It's lucky that dinosaur was here," An Dung said.

"You have a different concept of luck than me," Robin replied.

"Recall where that gator was sitting when it was grabbed?" An Dung said.

DeJuan saw his point. They were headed straight for the spot. "It feels a little eerie returning to the plane."

"How so?" asked Robin.

"I don't know." DeJuan thought about it for a moment. "I guess with knowing there are the bodies of the pilots still inside, it's like visiting a tomb."

They scrambled down to the lakeshore, but DeJuan hesitated as he neared the water's edge. Could there be another alligator hidden under the water? It seemed unlikely any would have stuck around after the sailback. Still, he dreaded going out into the lake. But they had no choice; he waded out. He stepped slowly through the water and tried not to make a wake. Watched around for any signs of movement.

Wakes. The others followed. Bill, Father O'Brien, and An Dung helped hoist him up onto the wing while Robin stayed on the shore and watched the water nearby for any disturbance.

"Help me up too," Father O'Brien insisted.

DeJuan raised his eyebrows at him. But after the priest stuck up his arms, DeJuan shrugged and grabbed the outstretched arms. Bill and An Dung got under Father O'Brien and helped hoist him up.

Bill and An Dung quickly jumped back out of the water and waited on the shore, away from its edge. DeJuan stuck his arms out for balance, not wanting to slip and fall back into the lake. Closer to the body of the plane, the wing was not as far above the water, but he had not even considered swimming out that far to climb aboard the wing. He stepped toward where the emergency exit door still hung open, wondering if anything had taken up residence inside. He glanced back at the spear he had left on the shore.

It was not a large opening though, so nothing much bigger than himself could have fit through. He peeked around the opening and over the seats, and not spotting any animals, stepped through the hatch. Then turned to help Father O'Brien.

DeJuan relaxed. Nothing seemed to be hidden inside. The front of the plane was mostly under water, but the floor had remained dry where they stood over the wing. He retrieved his bag from an overhead compartment nearby and examined inside it. The first aid kit was still there. He chastised himself for not having brought it along when they left the plane the first time.

Father O'Brien said a small prayer for the pilots stuck in their watery tomb, and then DeJuan and the father retrieved a few additional bags for other people. They retreated out the emergency exit and searched along the bank. There was no sign of the sailback returning, so they trotted to the end of the wing while DeJuan struggled to slide his arms through the straps of his backpack. Once it was securely on his back, he slid off the end of the wing and dropped into the water with a splash and then quickly dashed ashore, glad to be out of the lake. Father O'Brien was right behind him.

Yelling shattered the quiet. High above them, Carlos stood and fended off a juvenile rex with his spear. The rex stepped toward him, and he jabbed at its neck with his spear. The rex retreated a step.

DeJuan scrambled over and picked up his spear. He turned to charge up the bank to defend Carlos.

But another juvenile rex appeared behind Carlos. It swung its jaws forward and chomped down on his shoulder.

"No!" Robin screamed. She picked up a stone and angrily flung it toward the rexes. It landed well short.

Carlos's spear slipped from his hands as he seemed stunned. The first juvenile rex lunged forward and chomped down around Carlos's hips. The two rexes shook their powerful heads and tore the man apart.

DeJuan turned away, horrified. Numbed.

"We've got to help them," Bill shouted.

Robin eyes were moist. "Can't! Too late. They're gone. We gotta get out of here."

Bill stared a moment longer and then pointed to the right. "Along the shore. Go!"

"Come on, Father. Now's not the time for prayer," Robin said. The priest was down on a knee as he mumbled a prayer for Carlos.

DeJuan turned back toward where the two rexes stood. "What about David?"

"There's nothing we can do for him now. He's probably already dead too. If not, it'll be up to him to find his way back. Wish it was different." Robin turned and scurried along the shore, avoiding getting close to the water.

DeJuan turned and followed the three already headed out. Father O'Brien picked up his spear and took up the rear. DeJuan tried to get the picture of what had just happened out of his head as he told himself to think logically and figure out what they needed to do. They needed to put distance between themselves and the monsters. And they needed to be alert to their surroundings. After four hundred yards of lakeshore had been put between them and the rexes, they stopped.

"This is as good a place as any to go up," Robin said.

"Wait a second," Bill said. "Those two rexes were hunting in tandem."

"Uh, yeah," Robin replied.

"We have been assuming rexes hunt solo, but as juveniles, it's now clear that's not always the case."

"That's obvious," DeJuan said. "I think they were stalking us for a while. I thought I heard something behind us when we were up in those woods. I bet they waited until we separated. It's possible David and Carlos were separated back there before they attacked. The same thing happened the first time we were coming from the plane. A rex stalked us until we were out in the open. I now think it was waiting for one of us to separate from the group, but we didn't. Then when we reached the clearing, it either had to attack or give up on us." He thought about when he stopped to pick up that tooth in the woods. He had started to fall behind, but the flight attendant, Freeda, had come back to check on him. Had she saved his life back then? He would have to make sure to thank her when they got back.

"What's your point?" Bill asked.

"I think his point is we stick together and don't let anyone fall behind," Father O'Brien said.

"Next time you hear something behind us, don't keep it to yourself." Robin stared at DeJuan.

"I'm always hearing something behind us in the woods," DeJuan said.

Robin sighed and turned around. "Okay, no one falls behind. Let's head out."

"First I would like to say a prayer," Father O'Brien said. When everyone sighed and gave him a look that questioned the need for still another prayer, he seemed to have felt a need to explain. "I was praying for safe passage of Carlos's soul back there. Now I would like to pray for our safe passage through these woods. Humor me. I'm a little shaken."

"I don't think it'll hurt to pray for this." Bill bent down to his knees. An Dung joined him.

After they got to their feet, Bill turned to An Dung, "I thought your people were Buddhists. Did you convert?"

"My people?"

"You are Vietnamese?"

"I am." An Dung pulled out a cross on a chain from under his shirt. "And I'm Catholic. And my sister is Catholic. My parents are Catholic. My grandparents were Catholic. During the French colonial days, many missionaries came to Vietnam. Today, many Vietnamese are Catholic."

"Catholics, Protestants, Buddhists, Muslims, atheists, or whatever you are, it's time to get hiking," Robin said.

"Amen," Father O'Brien said.

"Father, tell me what you think." DeJuan needed to think about anything other than what he just witnessed. His thoughts turned to religion for reasons he didn't understand. "This obviously is not our universe. It must be some type of parallel or alternate universe. Maybe, there are many more universes. Do each have their own heaven?"

"There can be only one heaven since there is only one God."

DeJuan hiked in silence for a while as he pondered. "Okay. Let's say for argument's sake another parallel universe has another me. Suppose this other me, goes out and does horrific things, maybe like multiple murders. This version of me though is pious and does all the right things in life. Do I get to go to Heaven?"

Father O'Brien took several steps before he answered. "I don't think that would be possible."

"I don't get to go to Heaven?"

"Not what I meant," Father O'Brien laughed. "I mean I don't think it's possible for there to be two different versions of you. Your soul would have to be split between the different versions, and I don't believe it would be possible. There may be other universes other than the two we know about, and some may even have people, but they would not be the same people in each universe. But then again, what do I know?"

"Interesting."

"Why do you ask? I thought you didn't believe in God. Is this just theoretical or are you coming 'round?"

"No, Father. I don't believe the stories of the Bible or any other religious scriptures for that matter."

"Nor do I."

"I thought you had to believe in it."

Father O'Brien smiled. "I'm a Jesuit priest. We are free thinkers, my son, working for the greater glory of God. God's soldiers, if you will. I don't believe the world was formed in seven days 10,000 years ago, nor that everyone came from Adam and Eve. Science has proven otherwise. As I read the Bible, I am looking for the messages behind the stories. The Bible is the blueprint on how we should lead our lives, and we must reconcile it with what is in our hearts. But tell me, what do you believe?"

DeJuan shrugged. "I believe in what I can see and what I can measure. However ..."

"Yes? Go on."

"Well ... I find it astonishing this universe is so perfectly tuned for life."

"Perfectly tuned?"

"Actually, the universe has only small niches where complex life like us may form. But even that's only possible because matter can come together to form molecules and stars and planets. Change a single physical parameter such as the cosmological constant or the amount of dark energy or sizes or charges of subatomic particles just a little bit and we would have a universe in which none of this would be possible. Life as we know it wouldn't exist."

"Life as we know it," Father O'Brien repeated.

"Well yeah, maybe some other type of life would be possible. But it might have to be energy-based, not chemically based. And we don't know if such a life form is even possible."

"Do you believe then that there was a creator that made the universe?"

"Not necessarily. There is also the possibility that we are in one of an infinite number of universes, each with different parameters, and we just happen to be in the one that is suitable for life."

"Ah … the anthropic principle. Only we can ponder why the laws are so perfect because we live in the perfect one."

DeJuan was quiet for a minute before he continued, "There is another possibility though. Perhaps the universe itself is alive, and it or a progenitor universe created the parameters that are so conducive for life."

"To what purpose?"

"To study itself. We are just a small part of the universe. But we essentially are the universe trying to understand itself."

"What do you believe then?"

"I don't know what to believe. I don't have enough data and probably never will. I do wonder if there is some purpose to all this though. I would like to believe there is. It seems we all need to have some purpose to our lives."

"Then there is hope for you." Father O'Brien gently patted him on the back. "There is still hope, and all you need is a little faith."

Chapter 15 - DeJuan

The skyway between the mall and the remains of the East Parking Ramp had fast become the indoor place to eat or hang out. The parking ramp's fifth, sixth and seventh levels were the outdoor places with the seventh level open to the sky. Furniture and display racks had been tossed down the two stairwells which led from the third level of the parking ramp to the fourth until each were totally impassable mountains. Then someone decided the concrete floors just didn't have enough ambiance, so area rugs were brought to cover sections of the sixth level. Furniture and other decorum were added. The uncoordinated collection of patterns gave the level a very eclectic appearance, but it was a dinosaur-free zone. And there was far more seating than there were people at the mall.

DeJuan sat at a table on the sixth level, along with the others he now considered his new friends, while he stabbed his fork into the last piece of what had been a stack of pancakes smothered with syrup.

"Well, look who's back from the dead," Robin said.

Alanna escorted Joel to the table. "His fever broke. Be careful, though. He's still a bit cranky." Joel chuckled at the remark as Alanna turned and headed for the food line for the two of them. The rest all had empty plates in front of them and sipped on coffee, thanks to a French press.

"You're looking much better," Bill said.

"Alive anyway, thanks to all of you." Joel sat at their table. "This is quite the view." The outer wall of the ramp was missing, allowing him to stare off into the distance out of the wide-open end. He squinted. "Well, that's new."

Everyone turned. A herd of dinosaurs plodded across the open field to the east. Eight brontos, six enormous adults and two juveniles in the middle of them. DeJuan had insisted they were called *Brownstasaurus*, but no one seemed to listen to him about the name. Two large rexes trailed behind the brontos.

"They're going south," DeJuan said. "A larger group like that all going south can only mean they are starting to migrate."

"I don't get it. Why aren't the rexes attacking?" Bill asked.

"They won't attack the full-grown brownstasaurs," DeJuan said. "I suspect the adults are able to fend off the rexes, unless they're hurt or sick. The rexes are waiting for a chance to get at one of the younger ones or an adult that becomes sick. See how the brownstasaurs keep the juveniles in the middle of the group. What I find interesting though is there're two rexes, and they're not fighting each other for territory.

Apparently, the rexes have a complicated behavioral pattern. Maybe it depends on the season or the nature of the prey. Maybe other factors."

"That's our DeJuan," Robin said. "Never give a short answer when a lecture will do."

DeJuan wasn't sure if he had just been complimented or insulted, but everyone chuckled, and he joined along half-heartedly.

"We already know juveniles will cooperate sometimes," Bill said.

"I think the two out there are mates," DeJuan said. "It looks like one is limping a bit as it walks."

"I'm going to find some binoculars," Robin said. She got up and left the group.

"That's bird-like," DeJuan said. "Many birds pair bond, often for life." He thought back to the dead body the rex had carried away instead of eating a few days prior. Had it carried the body to its wounded mate? This one perhaps?

They watched the parade as Alanna came back with two plates stacked with pancakes and cut fruit. "Eat," she ordered Joel. "You need to get your strength back."

"Have any of you thought about where we are?" DeJuan asked.

"We know where we are. Where are you going with this?" Joel asked.

"I think this is most likely the same world as where the Brown's Station dinosaurs originated."

"Maybe, but so what if it is?" Joel asked.

"Then it's likely the people from Brown's Station are in this world with us. I think that we should try to make contact."

"The only way to be sure though would be for a team to go down there. That's well over a hundred miles from here," Joel said. "And this world doesn't have roads."

"Yeah, I know. It would be on the river though, so whoever went could go by boat."

Joel frowned. "And if there is no one there, then they would have to get all the way back up here by paddling against the current."

"Even if this is the same world, there might not even be anyone alive down there," Bill said. "The dinosaurs have gotten how many of us already?"

Alanna returned with glasses filled with juice. "If none are alive, I hate to think what that implies about our chances." She must have overheard them as she returned.

"They don't have a mall like this for protection," Joel said.

"True," DeJuan said. "But they would have other buildings. Perhaps schools, commercial buildings, or churches that are big enough to hide them from the dinosaurs. And they would have had all the supplies of their town, including the stores and their homes. They probably would have generators and gasoline. Most importantly, they would have guns. I think they survived. At least many of them."

"I think it's too risky," Joel said.

DeJuan glanced at Joel. He thought Joel was being risk adverse because two people had died getting medicine for him. Maybe even felt guilt about it, and he didn't want to risk more lives. "All right, let's analyze this."

Robin and Bill groaned.

Why did they do that every time he used the word *analyze*? DeJuan ignored them though. "There are three possibilities. One, no one is there. I think that is the lowest probability though. Two, there is a community down there and they're doing better than us with supplies to get them through the winter."

"There is enough here to get us through the winter," Joel said.

"True. But three. There're people down there, but they're in real trouble, and they'd be better off here."

DeJuan was pretty sure he knew how Joel would consider this last scenario. His doctrine was to not leave anyone behind. Help those who needed help.

"Okay, suppose I was to lead an expedition down to the Brown's Station—" Joel said.

Alanna turned and jabbed a finger at Joel. "Whoa! Stop right there, mister. You're in no shape to be going anywhere anytime soon."

"I agree. You shouldn't be doing anything strenuous for at least a week," DeJuan said.

"Why thank you for the advice, Doctor Jazkins." Joel smiled.

"You're welcome." DeJuan wondered why Joel had stressed *doctor*.

"If there's an expedition down to Brown's Station, we should get a radio system set up. A ham radio would have enough range I should think." Joel apparently was not totally ruling out leading the expedition.

"Where do we get one of those?" DeJuan asked.

"This is a huge mall. There must one in one of these stores."

"First things first, guys," Alanna said. "You're going to need a boat or something. I don't recall seeing any of those anywhere in this mall."

DeJuan set his fork down. "But we should be able to make something that floats reasonably well."

"The boat will have to return too," Joel replied.

"Maybe, but so?"

"It will have to be a boat that's easy enough to paddle against the current."

"What boat?" Robin asked. Having just returned with three sets of binoculars, she handed sets to Joel and DeJuan. DeJuan took a quick peek through his set at the parade still within sight and then passed the set to Camila.

Bill said, "They've been discussing a trip down the river to see if any of the Brown's Station people are still there."

"Count me in. Who else is going?" Robin asked.

"We haven't decided yet if anyone's going," Joel replied.

"I'll go if needed," DeJuan said. "But I'm sure others are more qualified who might be willing to go. The outdoors is not really something I have much experience with. Lack of volunteers isn't the problem though. Lack of a boat is."

"There's a wooden canoe, and maybe even paddles, up on the wall of The Northwoods," Robin said. "I don't know if it floats, but we could patch it up if needed."

"Northwoods? Is that an outdoor store?" DeJuan asked.

"It's a restaurant, not a store. Down on the first level," Joel answered. Then he turned to Robin. "You seem to know what's in every restaurant here."

Robin shrugged. "I eat out a lot. Whenever my family comes to visit, we eat out someplace new here at the mall." Robin suddenly appeared sad. DeJuan wondered if she missed her family already.

"How was the food here?" DeJuan asked.

"Really good," Robin replied. "I had batter-fried walleye and wild rice with lingonberry sauce on the side. A glass of white wine, the one time I was here."

Bill stood with them just inside the entrance to The Northwoods. The interior was dark, but above where the maître d' would have been asking them "how many," a canoe and paddles were stuck up against the wall along with a bunch of other outdoor memorabilia. With a flashlight in hand, Bill fetched a chair from a nearby table.

DeJuan winced and wrinkled his nose. "Whew! It smells in here."

"Rotten meat." Bill pinched his nose.

"And fish," Robin added.

"Yeah, all these restaurants down here really have a bad odor." DeJuan stepped toward the table to grab his own chair.

"And it's not the type of odor that grows on you," Bill said.

"Ewe! Or maybe it does," Robin said. "We shouldn't touch anything without gloves."

"We'll be all right without them as long as we don't go back into the kitchen," DeJuan said.

Bill stepped onto his chair. "Hey, we got a problem here. A really big problem."

"What are you talking about?" Robin asked.

Bill replied, "We don't have a canoe."

"What?" DeJuan cried.

"We have half a canoe. It looks like it was sawed in half before it was mounted on the wall. Actually, I don't think it's even a real canoe."

"Shit!" Robin cursed. "I should have seen that."

"Authentic or not, the paddles at least look like they're serviceable," Bill said. "I am going to need some type of saw, maybe a hack saw, to cut those free. They seem to be stuck down with epoxy. Sears should have a saw. I'll run over there."

"Those paddles won't do us any good without a boat," Robin said. "We'll be up a creek with a boat."

"We'll figure something out," DeJuan said.

"Give DeJuan your flashlight," Robin said. "We'll stay here and look for anything else that might be useful."

"Looking for anything in particular?" DeJuan asked. Bill already headed for the door.

Bill turned and tossed his flashlight to DeJuan. "Stuff for the trek. Maybe fishing or camping gear."

"How long is this trip going to take?" DeJuan swung the flashlight up along the wall near the bar and spotted a rod and reel.

"You said it's about 140 miles, right?" Robin asked.

"Yeah, about."

"Maybe five days. No. I am forgetting about current. Probably four days, but that would be in a canoe. I am basing this all on my experience of canoeing through the boundary waters. It could take longer if we have to use some type of boat or raft," Robin answered.

"Raft!" An idea popped into DeJuan's head. "I think I know how we could build a nice sturdy one."

"How?" Robin eyes shot toward the door. "Shush! Did you just hear that?"

"Bill's probably coming back."

"Too soon! And it didn't sound like him."

They both grabbed their spears and crept toward the front entrance. The doors had been kept open to let more light into the restaurant.

A large shadow appeared in the doorway, and they both froze. The shadow was of a head full of huge, pointed teeth.

DeJuan felt a tap on his shoulder and turned to see Robin point toward the back. He tip-toed with her as she ducked behind the bar.

It was the rotting meat which drew the monster inside. He silently cursed to himself; they were so stupid to come down without a radio or a watcher above the open mall entrance to warn them.

They peered over the bar through a set of tall glass mugs. When the rex stuck its head through the doorway, its image was distorted by the curvature of the mugs, but DeJuan could easily tell it was a juvenile. The beast stood about eight feet tall. The spikes along its back scraped the top of the door frame as it stepped into the waiting area.

It stopped halfway into the establishment and snorted. Then a second snort. The rex had sniffed the air. DeJuan hoped it had not smelled them and would go for the odorous meat and fish in the back where the kitchen was located.

The beast stepped forward into the dining area. As its body squeezed through, tables and chairs tumbled and clattered to the floor. The rex appeared indeed to be headed for the kitchen, and maybe they could make their escape once it went past.

But then it stopped right next to the bar instead. Another snort. Shit! DeJuan hadn't showered since they arrived, and he stunk to the high heavens as they all did.

A red color to his right caught his eye. He slowly laid his spear down on the floor in front of him.

The rex stepped forward, and crashing noises came as its tail whipped around, and then more chairs crashed to the floor. Its head slowly crept over the top of the bar, starting with the tip of its snout.

Robin thrust her spear upward into the bottom of its jaw.

DeJuan rolled out to the side instead, and, in the next instant, he popped the pin out of the fire extinguisher next to them. He jumped to his feet and blasted a large cloud of cold carbon dioxide directly into the snout of the rex.

The rex recoiled back and tumbled, crashing through tables and chairs. Several burst into splinters. The beast screeched as it up-righted itself and then scrambled to squeeze itself out through the exit. It turned and disappeared toward the open end of the mall.

"Let's get out of here!" DeJuan hands shook as he set the fire extinguisher down.

"Yeah! Careful though," Robin said. "There could be a another one out there." DeJuan knew she was right. They now knew rexes sometimes hunted in pairs.

DeJuan followed Robin to the exit. Her head darted around before she raced across to the nearby escalator. DeJuan glanced at the trail of blood droplets before also dashing for the escalator.

With a team of guards and watchers, Robin, Bill, and DeJuan returned later to cut the paddles free. Then they pulled out a large table, removed its legs and carried it over to Sears. DeJuan instructed members of the ad-hoc team to find large plastic tub containers while he found bathtub stickers. He returned to the table and decorated the top with orange, white, and black clownfish. It made the table look like a kid's table, but it would keep Robin and Bill from sliding off when it got wet.

"What the hell?" Bill had returned and stared down at the table . "Really? Clownfish?"

"I could peel them off and stick on the yellow duckies I found instead," DeJuan offered.

Bill shook his head as he walked away, leaving Robin laughing at his back. After Bill was gone, Robin had DeJuan replace one of the fish with a ducky.

DeJuan then attached wooden strips along each edge to create a lip so if something slid or rolled on the raft, it could catch on the lip. Once the others returned with the plastic containers, DeJuan attached them to the bottom of the table with epoxy and made sure all the gaps between the lids and the tubs were sealed. He designed it with larger containers along the left and right edges and smaller containers in the center which gave it a bit of a pontoon or catamaran profile. He thought it might be easier to paddle and maneuver with his design. Finally, he added a small make-shift rudder to the back.

It was too late in the day for the journey to begin, so they took the raft over to the Log Chute, a water ride in the amusement park in the center of the mall and left it there. Water remained in the basin, and the next day they would test the raft to make sure it floated high enough once Robin and Bill and their supplies were loaded on top. The extra time would also insure the epoxy fully cured.

Chapter 16 - DeJuan

The next morning, DeJuan sat at what had become their usual table for breakfast. On his plate were sausage patties and pancakes covered in syrup, and a cup of coffee rested next to the plate.

"Enjoy that sausage, boys," Robin said. "Heard this is the last of it."

DeJuan didn't mind so much. The pancakes were good too. But perhaps he would get tired of them over time. There were other choices though like dry cereal or energy bars.

"So much food here that had just gone to waste. It's a shame we don't have refrigeration," Bill said.

"We didn't appreciate it until we didn't have it anymore," Alanna said.

"Like a lot of things," DeJuan added.

"We need to start thinking about how to get some dinos for the grill," Robin said.

"You want to go hunting them down?" Bill stared at her.

"Well … yeah!" she replied. "Eventually, the meat in the freezers will eventually all turn to rot. We'll still have to eat."

"What are we going to use to kill them? Our spears?" Bill asked. "Like something out of an old B movie."

"Maybe we should start thinking about how to set a trap for one," DeJuan said.

Bill squinted. "Is today Friday?"

"It is only Wednesday," Alanna replied.

Bill counted on his fingers. "So today is the fifth day since we got poofed here. Seems like way longer."

"Why are you suddenly so focused on how long we've been here?" Robin asked.

"Just curious," Bill replied. "I wondered how many days it took for you all to go crazy."

"Can't speak for DeJuan, but I'm just as sane as before the poofing," Robin said.

"If we are here a whole year, do we designate a day in October of next year as Poofing Day?" DeJuan asked.

"Not celebrating that day," Bill said.

Joel switched topics and went straight to business. "What about the radio?"

They had looked all over the mall, but all they could find were battery operated shortwave receivers. No transmitters. Then one of the custodians thought there was a radio with a transmitter in one of the corporate offices that he regularly cleaned. It turned out Mr. Forthwain was a collector of old aviation items and displayed them in a case in his office.

"Had a tag that said ARC dash five," DeJuan said. "It's a really old aircraft radio, appears to have been military. In fact, it is so old it actually has vacuum tubes in it."

"Does it work though?" Joel asked.

"Yeah, but it took some fiddling. Top had a plate on it that reads 28-volt CW."

"CW?" Joel asked.

"Continuous wave."

"Ah," Joel uttered.

"What?" Alanna asked.

"Continuous wave means we will be communicating in Morse code," Joel replied.

"Right," DeJuan said, impressed Joel knew what the letters meant. "There was a booklet in his office that had the Morse code key, so Camila took the time to make a copy."

"Good. We will have a copy of the code with us then," Bill said.

"Yeah, played hooky during that course in school," Robin said. It had been decided Robin and Bill would the two on the raft.

"The tricky part was the 28 volts," DeJuan said.

"That sounds like an odd voltage. Why did they have to go and mess with things like that?" Robin asked.

"Increasing the voltage allowed them to use less copper in the wires to carry the current," DeJuan replied. "Lowered the weight of the plane. Anyway, I was looking down in Sears for a converter, and I came across the power tools. It turns out the batteries many of the portable power tools run on are 28 volts. I grabbed a couple of those. They come pre-charged, and, voila, we have a transmitter."

"I think you should transmit each day right at seventeen hundred hours," Joel said to Robin and Bill.

"What time is that? I always get confused with military time," Bill said.

"Five o'clock," Joel replied. "If you can't send a message for some reason—"

"Like we're being chased by a rex?" Robin said.

"Let's hope that's not the reason. But if you can't at five because of delays, then exactly at six. We'll be listening for your signal at those times. It can be just a short message like 'all OK, 80 miles downriver.' Just so we know you're okay and where about you're at. Wait one minute and then repeat your message exactly, so we can be sure we got it right."

"Suppose we don't see anything. We're bringing a map, but the land may look different than the map. At what point should we give up and turn around?" Robin asked.

Joel said, "Use your best guess of how far you've traveled based on your speed. If you hit 200 miles and still don't see any signs of people, turn around. Let's go over your provisions."

"Everything's in sealed plastic bags in case we're rained on or someone happens to kick it overboard," Robin said.

"Hey! Am I to imply you think I'm clumsy?" Bill asked.

"You would be inferring, actually," DeJuan corrected.

Robin ignored them both. "We've plenty of food and enough bottled water for five days. The food and water will be trailing us in a cooler tied to the raft. If we're forced to return, we'll have to do it mostly survival style, although we'll have a few protein bars left. We have our spears, spare knives, and a machete. We're bringing a tent and a pair of sleeping bags, a couple of ultralight hammocks, butane lighters and a pot to cook in or boil water in if we need to. We're bringing one fishing pole we scavenged from down at The Northwoods and a few extra lures, bug spray, some extra rope for cordage, a small foldable camping shovel and a small flashlight with spare batteries. Most of our gear is going in the two storage boxes to make sure it stays dry. We'll also be using those for seats."

"Bring along a couple rolls of tp also," Joel said. "Besides for the obvious, it makes for good fire-starting material if everything else is damp."

"When are you leaving?" Alanna asked.

"Right after this breakfast we're going down to test the raft and make sure it floats." Robin sipped the last of her coffee. "If everything looks good, then we're taking it over to the river right after that."

It wasn't right after breakfast. While they were sipping their coffee, a large rex had entered the mall. It was too large to go into any of the restaurants from where the rotten odor of the decaying meat that had lured it into the mall in the first place originated, so the rex circled around and around the first level of the mall. At first, everyone thought they could just wait it out since they figured eventually the monster would get frustrated and leave.

After two hours of the rex circling the first level, people got impatient and a little bored with the rex, improbable as it seemed. Some decided to act. For the next hour, people dropped heavy or sharp objects from the third level down onto the rex in attempts to kill it, hurt it or at least annoy it enough to cause it to leave. Unfortunately, it was hard to aim a falling desk, and the rex was almost always a moving target. Some threw baseballs at it and loud cheers erupted when they hit it, but the rex didn't even seem to notice. A few times it was hit with something heavier like a steel chair, and it became annoyed enough to roar up at the perceived thrower of the item but not annoyed enough to leave the mall.

Some people thought it would be funny to paint the dinosaur, so they found gallons of paint. Purple paint, and they gave the rex a name, Barney. DeJuan thought there must be a reason for the name, but he didn't get it. Probably had some culturally connection from music or television. DeJuan had hardly watched any television his entire life.

DeJuan came up with an idea for luring the purple dinosaur out of the mall. Someone would have to go down to the first level, using the escalator right by the open hole, and leave a trail of rotten meat to the outside. Since it was his idea, he was persuaded into being the meat man.

When the rex was at the opposite corner of the mall, DeJuan raced down the escalator and out toward the opening. He tossed several packages in a line from the opening back toward him and then raced back to the escalator.

"Whew!" He sniffed his arms. Some of the packages had dripped, and now he smelled almost as bad as the meat. As he climbed the escalator steps, others tossed more packages out of the openings at the end from the second and third levels. The rex turned the corner and lumbered down the walkway just as DeJuan reached the safety of the second level. He scooted forward to where he could watch the giant strut past as the rex marched down the hall toward him.

The rex stopped right below him and snorted. It turned its gigantic head sideways and peered up at him. Damn, the creature had a heck of a good sense of smell. It stared right at DeJuan with one giant eye, and DeJuan felt his skin crawl. Could the beast somehow reach up and get him?

DeJuan breathed a sigh of relief as the rex stepped forward again and stooped. It picked up a package of the odorous meat and lifted its head to swallow. The paper wrapping, along with the meat, went down into its gullet. Then the rex stepped to the next package and then the next, on a trail to the outside. Out in the sunlight, the rex dined on a pile of well over a hundred pounds of decaying meat before it strutted toward the south.

As the giant beast left, a few people waved and held bottles of wine or brandy while they sang wildly and out of tune to the departing purple dinosaur. After they sang something about the dinosaur loving them too they burst out hooting and howling. DeJuan couldn't see what was so darn funny.

He peered down at his arms and then scrunched up his nose. The odor on his arms from the rotten meat was awful, and the rest of him didn't smell so good either. It had been a long time since he had last bathed. He found a couple of really soft bath towels, a pair of swim trunks, a bottle of shampoo and a bar of soap while he browsed through a couple of stores. Then he asked Father O'Brien to watch over the southeast opening for a while as he went down to a wishing pond in the southwest corner of the central court. And had a bath. It felt a little strange as he sat in the water, coins under his bottom and exposed for all the others to watch. He soon stopped caring though as he lathered himself with soap and turned the water around him sudsy. Others watched from above, and soon he was joined by many others for a bath party. As he left to dry off and relieve Father O'Brien, still others jumped in.

Chapter 17 - DeJuan

Bill and Robin chose to wait until the following morning to depart which allowed them to get a full day's push on the river before they settled down somewhere for the night. DeJuan joined the group who accompanied them east to the Minnesota River. He was among several who together carried the raft and the supplies. Others carried spears, along for protection against raptors or juvenile rexes. If a large rex or sailback appeared, they would have to try to get to some type of cover because they would not be able fend off one of them in the open.

Joel insisted he felt better and came along also on the two-mile journey. The trip was uneventful though; not a single carnivorous dinosaur of any species was seen on the trip to the river nor on the return to the mall.

It was DeJuan's first time through the woods without the feeling of being followed. He wondered if the absence of dinosaurs was because most had migrated away from the area or if they were just having a lucky day.

It was early afternoon. They had decided as a group all spoiled and questionable food had to be tossed. It was beginning to smell mighty unpleasant throughout the mall, and the foul smell was an invitation to rexes and other dinosaurs. Maybe the aroma was also more noticeable since they had all bathed. Some spoiled food had already been tossed, but it had been limited to the kitchens raided at the time for food. This was to be a systematic cleansing, and at the same time, all good meat still frozen or cold would be moved to the best freezers on the third level. DeJuan pointed out stocking all the frozen or cold items together in one or two spots would have the advantage of slowing down the thawing process, so less of it would go to waste.

"Man, this stuff stinks," DeJuan tossed another package of ground beef into the custodial cart and let the blood from the package drip off his rubber gloves and into the cart.

"Should've brought clothespins for our freaking noses," An Dung said. "I don't think we can lift more than this. Time to take this load out and dump it."

They hauled the cart to the nearest escalator, and DeJuan tilted it. DeJuan wished the escalator ran. But together they dragged the cart up, step after step, until they reached the top. There they stopped to catch their breaths before they pushed the cart to the West Parking Ramp.

Others with spears watched for them from there in case something decided to come up the ramp. DeJuan and An Dung pushed their cart across to the west side and peered over. Below were two juvenile rexes, the reason DeJuan and An Dung had to come up to the second level to dump. The rexes buried their long snouts into what had been dumped earlier in the afternoon. It hadn't taken long for them to find the decaying meat.

"Are they still there?" Joel asked. He and Alanna pulled another cart toward them.

"Oh yeah! I don't think much is going to budge them unless a big rex comes around," DeJuan replied. He and An Dung tossed packages from their load to the left of the rexes. The rexes lifted their heads when they heard the packages plop on the ground, and then they tilted their heads up toward the crowd above them. Just as quickly, they dug their blood-covered snouts back into the pile in front of them.

Joel and Alanna pushed their cart up next to DeJuan and An Dung's cart and tossed more packages. Still more packages dropped from above them; others cleansed the third and fourth levels.

Soon, they declared the dirty job finished. Many people along the wall gazed down at the spectacle of the feeding rexes. DeJuan noticed a woman up on the third level used her phone to record the spectacle. He was surprised the woman's phone still had a charge. Perhaps she had it turned off before or had recharged it from a car.

Below, the rexes were joined by a third juvenile, and they moved over to the new pile of packaged meat. One of them lifted its head and peered up at them. It was the same one who had looked at him before. Was the rex thankful to them for the packages, or had it just eyed him for desert? DeJuan found its stare to be unnerving.

"This takes me back to the day we got poofed. I was up on that ramp over there." Alanna pointed at what was left of the highway overpass ramp. "I looked down and saw a rex tearing the roof off a car. That was a much bigger rex though."

"It must have been terrifying," DeJuan said.

"Oh, it was awful! It was dark, and the next thing I knew there was this gigantic monster roaring up at me from practically under my feet. I'd never been so terrified in my entire life. I almost blacked out I was so scared." She shuddered. Joel put his arm around her, and she gently leaned on his shoulder. "I wish I could forget that morning. First it was those two cars flying off the end of the ramp, and there was nothing I could do to stop them. At least then those guys in the third car stopped."

Joel removed his arm from around Alanna.

Alanna turned and looked at Joel with concern. "Joel? What's wrong?"

"Those guys who took our swords. Their car was the third car to leave the mall?" Joel asked.

"Yeah. So?" asked Alanna.

"What's going on?" DeJuan was now alarmed by Joel's reaction too.

"Those guys said the Chicago gang shot Emilio," Joel said. "But that doesn't fit with their car being the last up the overpass since the shooter was in the last car to leave the ramp."

"Maybe the shooters passed them on the way down," Alanna said.

"Maybe." Joel didn't seem convinced. "What make of car did they drive?"

Alanna shook her head. "I don't know. It was dark, and I didn't get a good look at it. It was a sedan, but so were the other two that flew off the ramp."

"I don't suppose anybody knows where their car is now," Joel said.

"Nobody's seen it as far I've heard," DeJuan said. That was strange too he realized now that he thought about it.

"Where could it be?" Joel asked. "It's not on this parking ramp or the north side of the mall. We would have seen it. The same goes for the upper levels of the east side."

"They couldn't have gotten up to those levels anyway because the parking ramp would have been gone by the time they came back from the highway," DeJuan said.

"That leaves two spots." Joel dashed to the southeast corner of the parking ramp; Alanna and DeJuan followed behind. Joel peered toward the mall. "Not on this side. So, that leaves only the first level on the other side." Joel's hands turned into clenched fists at his side. "I have to go check it out."

"Why is this so important?" Alanna huffed from trying to catch up.

"I saw the car leaving after Emilio was shot. I know the taillights. The last number on the plate."

"Is this such a good idea?" Alanna asked. "Remember they have a gun."

"Haven't forgotten."

"But you're going to go looking for them anyway." Alanna bit her lower lip.

Joel nodded. "I have to know." He turned and immediately headed for the mall entrance.

"I'm going with you," DeJuan said.

Alanna grabbed DeJuan's arm and stared at him. "Don't let him do anything foolish. Please."

Joel and DeJuan reached the first level of the East Parking Ramp, and Joel charged through. There was only one car, parked toward the north side of the structure. Joel sprinted to the car, a blue Honda Civic; DeJuan raced after him.

"Is this the car?" DeJuan asked.

"No," Joel replied as he walked up to it. He opened the unlocked driver side door, reached across, and popped open the glove box. He flipped through some papers and then shoved them all back in. "It's Alanna's."

"What do we do then?"

Joel scratched his head. "We've been on every level on the West Parking Ramp and this is the only level possible on this side. Pretty obvious their car isn't here at the mall."

"Do you think it's over at Ikea?"

"The logical place to look. When we were there before, there were three cars in the lot. We assumed those were the employee's cars, but maybe we were wrong. I never saw the backs of them."

"If we're heading back to Ikea, I think we should get a few more people to tag along," DeJuan said. "I'd bet An Dung would volunteer."

"All right, but don't mention this to Father O'Brien."

DeJuan nodded. If there was revenge involved, the priest wouldn't approve and would almost certainly try to talk them out of taking any action. It was clear Joel didn't want to be talked out of anything, and DeJuan wondered what anything might include. Hopefully, nothing foolish.

Half an hour later DeJuan stood in the Ikea parking lot beside Joel as they stared at the backs of the three cars in the lot all parked near each other in the same corner. DeJuan glanced upward for a moment. The sky had been overcast most of the day, but it seemed to have gotten darker. An Dung and L'Troy kept anxiously looking around. DeJuan couldn't blame them if they wondered what monsters might be hidden in the woods on the other side of the highway. He wondered too.

"Any of these the one?" DeJuan asked.

"No." Joel shook his head and then marched to the nearest car, a black sedan, and, after he tried the passenger side door handle, turned his hand-made spear around. Thunder rumbled from the west as he rammed the wood butt of his spear through the passenger side window. He glanced in the direction of the thunder. Then he reached over the broken glass and flipped the lock open. Inside the car, he rifled through the glove box.

"Registration says Mikel Roznovakovic." Joel stumbled over the last name. Camila had given Mikel as one of the names of the deceased for whom they didn't find a body. It wasn't Jimmy or Scar's car. He repeated the action for the other two cars and both belonged to people who had been co-workers of Camila. They marched up to the upper level of the parking lot, but no cars were parked there.

"Frick! Where the hell could it be?" Joel scanned along the highway to the west of them.

"Over there. We need to go look at those." DeJuan pointed toward just beyond where the highway ramp over the freeway ended to the northwest of them. After the poofing, that area had suddenly become dense woods with fifty-foot trees and deadfall which littered the ground.

"Looks like the cars of the Chicago gang," Joel said. "Of course. Good thinking."

Thunder again rolled across the darkening sky as the foursome scooted down the ramp, and it started to drizzle as they crossed the open space between the parking lot and the end of the overpass where the cars had crashed.

A black Cadillac was on its side. The other car, a black Impala, had its back end resting over the trunk of a large, downed tree. Both cars were total wrecks. The roofs had been torn off, and glass shards and other small pieces of jagged metal and splinters of plastic littered all over the dead leaves on the ground.

Beyond the cars, still up in a tree, a boat rested across a pair of big boughs. It was a small blue runabout with a V-shaped bow, but a large branch protruded through the stern. The vehicle which had towed it was not seen. The twisted trailer for the boat had somehow gotten separated and leaned against a tree trunk a little farther to the north. The lucky bastards must have made it over before the poofing caught their boat behind them in this world. Unless, the bridge collapsed under them, and they didn't survive. DeJuan realized it was possible he would ever know how their story ended.

L'Troy slapped his arm hard, and the sound echoed through the woods. All the others stared at him. "What? I was gettin' bit by a skeeto. Creatures always seem to like to eat me."

The others glared at him for a moment longer to let him know he advertised their position.

"Are either of these the one?" DeJuan whispered.

Joel stared at the back of the Impala for a moment and shook his head. He marched around to the back of the Cadillac and again shook his head. Joel raised his head and stared DeJuan directly in the eye. They both thought the same thing. Jimmy was both a liar and a murderer. Lightning flashed and gave bright light to the whole area for a second.

DeJuan scrambled for cover as did everyone else. It wasn't the nearby lightning flash or the large boom of the thunder a second later. The bright flash revealed a large rex previously camouflaged and hidden in the dark of the woods twenty-five yards from them.

They all yelled to run about the same time. Joel dashed for the nearest columns which supported the overpass structure. An Dung followed.

DeJuan dove behind the Impala. L'Troy scrambled behind the giant root structure of the fallen tree which held up the Impala. DeJuan scrambled on his knees toward the tree trunk which elevated the rear of the car just far enough. He flipped onto his back and squeezed under the car.

The rex came to the Impala in a couple quick strides and lowered its snout to the ground next to the car just as DeJuan pulled his feet under. Then the giant moved around to the other side and snorted. The rex could not get down low enough to see with an eye, but it used its sense of smell. DeJuan felt warm jets of air blow past him with each snort. The creature's breath smelled almost as bad as the rotten hamburger they had tossed earlier.

The rex jostled the car with its snout and rocked it gently. Its snout banged hard into the side door, and the car slid a few inches down along the trunk. The rex banged it and pushed, and the car slid along the trunk a whole foot. DeJuan squirmed along under the tree trunk so the car was still over him. The ground sloped though, and the space got tighter. The rex tried to push a third time, but the Impala was up against what was left of a thick vertical branch. DeJuan hoped the rex wouldn't try to lift the car and push it away to get at him. It was probably strong enough. If the rex tried, there was also the chance the car would slip and crush him under it.

The rex snorted one more time and then turned its head toward Joel and An Dung as they fled away under the overpass ramp. It turned and charged their direction.

DeJuan pulled himself out and peeked over the tree trunk at the rex as it raced toward Joel and An Dung. DeJuan hoped those guys had enough of a head start.

Something touched his shoulder. He jumped back and banged his backside against the Impala. It was just L'Troy though.

"Shit! Say something first next time." DeJuan wiped his rain-soaked face on his sleeve.

"Didn't mean to give you a heart attack," L'Troy whispered. "I was trying to be quiet, so I didn't say nothing."

"Where were you?" DeJuan asked.

L'Troy pointed to the end of the downed tree. "Behind the roots there. Man, I've never been so scared in my entire stinkin' life. If that monster went there, it would have gotten me for sure. There's no stinkin' way I was gettin' away."

DeJuan caught sight of something shiny metallic on the ground. There were a lot of car pieces on the leaves, but this had a different look to it. He brushed the fallen leaves away and picked up the shiny barrel of a large revolver. "Know anything about guns?"

L'Troy shook his head. "Check it for bullets."

DeJuan could see from the outside it had bullets in the cylinder. "Says 357 on the barrel. But it has mud in the barrel. I know enough that if I try to shoot like this, it's going to explode. Gonna see if I can poke out the mud with a stick."

"Be careful not to shoot yourself."

"Go look in the cars and see if you can find any more guns," DeJuan said.

L'Troy searched while DeJuan cleaned the barrel of the revolver. L'Troy came back a minute later with a second gun, a pistol, he had found in the glove box of the Cadillac. "I found one more. No extra bullets. This one has a number nine on the barrel."

"Probably means 9 mm," DeJuan said. "Let's go back toward Ikea and then to the mall from there. I hope those guys are all right." He glanced toward the direction Joel and An Dung had dashed.

"Know that old joke: how fast do you have to run to escape from a bear?" L'Troy asked.

"Yeah. Faster than the guy next to you. Robin used that joke a couple of days after we arrived," DeJuan replied.

"Yup. Only I don't think it works for a monster like that." L'Troy pointed at where the rex disappeared. "It'd get both of us."

"Probably right." DeJuan nodded as the rain poured down on them. Again, he glanced toward where he had last seen Joel and An Dung.

Chapter 18 - Joel

An Dung stumbled over a branch and toppled to the ground. Joel stopped and retreated to pull him to his feet with his free arm; the other still clutched his make-shift spear. A quick glance back told him the rex had given up on the car wreck and had turned its attention to them. At least DeJuan and L'Troy were safe for now.

He and An Dung had to find safety somewhere soon though. He took a quick peek at the mall. If they headed in that direction, they would have to go around the parking ramp to reach an entrance. It was too far and too open; the rex would easily catch them before they were half-way across. He searched ahead.

"There!" He pointed to where the on ramp above them curved toward the mall and sloped down to ground level. He and An Dung sprinted toward the spot.

As they got closer, Joel spotted a black sedan hidden in the shadows, parked up under the ramp as far as it could go. It was dark under there, but Joel still recognized the rear taillights. The last number on the plate. He knew whose car it was.

His emotions were boiling over. Relieved for DeJuan and L'Troy. Hatred for the guys who killed Emilio, and he felt a strong desire for revenge. He also feared for his and An Dung's lives as the rex bore down on them. The rex was not far behind.

"Up under there." Joel pointed with his free hand, the other still swinging his spear as he ran.

They dashed past the car and climbed under the ramp. Squeezed as close as they could under where the ramp buttressed against the embankment.

The rex was too tall and its head too big to get close to them under the ramp, and the car was in its way as well. It used its snout and shoved the car over a foot and then snorted. Lightning flashed as the monster stomped around to the other side of the ramp, but it still couldn't reach them.

As the rex's snout got close, Joel slashed at it above its upper jaw with his spear. The rex didn't even flinch from the bleeding wound, but it gave a snort. It seemed to say it could still smell them in there, and now it was pissed off. The two scooted back to the other side under the ramp as far as they could crawl. The rex circled under the ramp to the other side, but Joel and An Dung again scooted away.

After a while, the rex appeared to give up, It turned and stomped back into the woods on the other side of the highway. At the edge of the thick growth of trees, it paused and stared at them before disappearing. Joel had the distinct impression there was some thought process behind the eyes of the monster.

It was several minutes before Joel and An Dung dared to move. They eased themselves out quietly and stared at the woods. Joel glanced behind them to be sure the rex (or some other creature) hadn't circled back on them.

His attention turned to the car as the driver's side front door slowly opened, and Jimmy Tones stepped out. Then the back door opened, and Scar appeared. Jimmy loosely held his revolver in one hand and the sword in the other. Scar also held a stolen sword. The pungent odor of pot smoke reached Joel's nose.

"Guess ya found our hideout," Jimmy said.

"It was you who shot Emilio," Joel growled. If Jimmy hadn't been holding the revolver, Joel would have immediately attacked him with his spear. He thought about it anyway. Considered throwing it at the man. He was sure his aim would be good, but Jimmy would shoot him while he was still in his wind-up. Jimmy and Scar were likely a little impaired, but it didn't take much coordination to fire a gun at close range. Besides, he would not be able to get them both with one toss. If he could only take down one of them though, it going to be Jimmy.

"Figured it just a matter of time 'fore someone figured id out," Jimmy said. "How ya do it?"

"The taillights on your car."

"Mm. Who else knows?"

"DeJuan and L'Troy know. Probably back at the mall by now," Joel replied. He thought Jimmy was trying to decide whether to shoot them or not. If the murderer didn't believe others knew, it was more likely. "Soon everyone will know."

An Dung squirmed in his shoes. "There's no need to shoot anyone."

"It's not everyone knowin' I did it dat stops my sleep," Jimmy said. "It's him." He tipped his sword toward Joel. "And dat bitch … ere, Robin. They'd cut my neck when I'm 'sleep. Them and maybe dat big dumb-lookin' one. It's dem I don't trust."

"Is that why you hid out here instead of sleeping in the mall with the rest of us?" Joel asked.

Jimmy gave a little affirmative grunt.

"So why haven't you shot me yet?"

"You askin' to have ya freaking brains blown out? Is dat what ya want? You sure stupid."

Joel stared at the man. If he were going to do it, then why hadn't he already? What held him back?

Joel noticed movement. The trees swayed behind the thugs. Something big came their way, and he was pretty sure he knew what. He reached his left hand out and grabbed An Dung's elbow as he took a step back and then another.

Jimmy finally decided to answer the question. "I've only so many bullets left. Haven't decided yet should I waste one on ya sorry ass." He looked puzzled as he watched them turn and run. "Oh, shit!" he cursed.

Joel glanced back. The rex appeared from out of the thick stand of trees and charged at Jimmy and Scar. Scar slipped and stumbled as he turned to run. Sprawled out onto the wet grass instead.

Jimmy raised his sword. but the rex's head swung down with its jaws open wide. Jimmy's arm fell away. The sword shattered across the rex's teeth.

Jimmy screamed. The rex's head bobbed again, and immense jaws clamped down around the man. Lifted him high off the ground. With a couple bobs of its head, it swallowed him whole.

Scar had scrambled back to his feet and ran toward Joel and An Dung. The rex took a couple of quick huge strides, and his giant leg crashed into Scar's back. Pinned the man down. Scar screamed for a second before being silenced. His body crushed.

Joel yelled to An Dung to follow him. There was no chance of making it to the mall in time if the rex decided two bodies wasn't filling enough. They ran instead in a circle around the bottom of the ramp and back under it again, so they were right back in the same spot they were at when they first hid from the rex.

The rain had stopped by then, and it seemed the darkness had lifted a little. The rex stomped past them and then stopped. It turned its head and stared straight at them tucked up under the ramp. It held Scar's lifeless body draped across its jaws. Then it turned and loudly stomped off into the woods. It was as if it said, "I'll be back for you later when I'm hungry again." Joel noticed how sometimes its movements were loud as if purposely announcing its presence to other animals. Other times it was very quiet as it hunted. The rexes were far more complicated creatures than they first appeared.

"Look!" An Dung pointed to where Jimmy had last stood. "His gun."

"Stay here," Joel said. He crept out and retrieved the revolver, the whole time his eyes on the woods where the rex had disappeared, and then he trotted back under the ramp.

"How many bullets are left?" An Dung asked.

Joel slid back the cylinder release latch and flipped the cylinder open. He dumped the shells into his hand. "None. These are all empty casings." Jimmy had used his last two bullets to murder Emilio and had bluffed the entire rest of the time. Joel felt foolish for haven fallen for it.

"Maybe there're some in the car," An Dung said.

Joel didn't answer. He knew if any were in the car, the gun wouldn't have been filled with empty casings. He thought about the way Jimmy never pointed the gun directly at anyone's face. He hadn't wanted anyone to see the empty chambers.

Joel glanced around and then stared at the car. "There won't be any bullets, but we should look anyway. Maybe there'll be something worth grabbing."

They found a trunk full of pot, but nothing of value to them. They found an ID for Randall Scarbrough, Scar's real name. Jimmy hadn't lied when he said it was the Chicago dudes that shot Emilio. Joel wondered where the two were from originally from, though, since people from Chicago didn't talk like Jimmy.

Joel thought they were safe from the rex for a while, so they hiked across toward the mall and on the way picked up the sword Scar had dropped. Joel wondered how Robin and Bill fared as he glanced at his watch. It was almost five.

Chapter 19 - Bill

Robin and Bill paddled at a steady pace. It had been mid-morning by the time they had pushed off and waved goodbye to those on shore. They kept to the strongest currents as best they could and allowed the river to do most of the work for them. Within about an hour, the Minnesota merged with the Mississippi as their raft continued to float northeast. The sky had turned overcast by then.

Around noon, the river began continuously curving in an arc toward the right until it flowed south. Robin and Bill ate a couple of protein bars and apples and continued down the river. As they floated, they eyed the clouds building up from the west; they hoped the rain held off. Occasionally, they stopped at small islands to relieve themselves and stretch their legs for a few minutes. They kept the breaks short since they wanted to reach the St. Croix River before setting up camp for the evening. At least that was the tentative plan. They were aware the geography might be different than on their old world, and the St. Croix might not even exist in the dinosaur world. But early signs were good with the geography being similar to what they knew and saw on their map. The

Mississippi and the Minnesota joined about where they should and then meandered northeast before it turned south just as it did in their old world.

Then the river widened into a lake just as the sky could no longer hold back. It started to drizzle on them, so they pulled out their ponchos. The drizzle slowly transformed into rain, and then they heard thunder off in the distance toward the west. They decided it wise to camp for the night. The last place they wanted to be was on the water when lightning struck.

Just off to their left was an island, several hundred yards long. They veered for it, beached their raft, and searched for a suitable camp site. Nothing ideal was found on the island. It was V-shaped with no spot more than about thirty feet from the water and much of it was nothing more than a big mud flat. But they had to pitch camp somewhere. They erected their tent on the highest point and draped the fly over it to keep them dry, and then Bill traipsed back in the steady rain and secured the rest of their gear. Robin gathered up what old fallen logs and branches she could find. The trees were few on the island, but enough lay around she had been able to start to encircle the tent with a wall of dead timber by the time Bill returned. She thought the ring of logs might keep the gators away from them in the night. Bill hoped she was right and helped her finish.

Despite the ponchos, their clothes were wet. Their socks were soaked through. Their pants were soaked up to the knees and the rest of their clothes were slightly damp as well. Robin ducked inside the tent and changed into a dry set of clothes first while Bill waited outside. Then Bill came in and changed while Robin pressed herself against one wall of the tent and promised not to peek. Bill was pretty sure she peeked anyway.

They hunkered down inside the tent and listened to the rain patter off the fly of their tent and on the nearby lake. They had hoped to build a fire and heat up a couple of cans of soup, something to warm their insides. Instead they dined on beef jerky, more protein bars, and apples, and they used their sleeping bags to warm themselves. At five, they sent the message as planned. It simply said "OK. ON ISLAND AT SPRING LAKE." and finished with the end of message sign. Then they repeated it a minute later. They had to trust the message was received back at the mall since communications were one-way.

Bill awoken by a tapping on his shoulder. He lifted his head, still turned away from Robin. "What is it?"

"Shush. There's something out there," Robin whispered. She was sitting upright. "Listen."

Suddenly fully awake, Bill rolled over into a sitting position next to her, still in his sleeping bag. The rain no longer patted the tent. Bugs chirped, and frogs croaked in the night. He was about to tell her it was just frogs when he heard a grunting noise. Not very loud, and it was hard to judge its distance or even its exact direction because of its low pitch. But the sound came from somewhere off to their left. He reached over and picked up his spear. "What do you think it is?"

"Don't know. Gator, maybe," she whispered back. "What if it's a sailback? I have no idea what they sound like."

"Just keep quiet and try not to move," he whispered.

Together, they sat in the pitch blackness of the inside of the tent and silently listened to the weird noises. With his sight gone, Bill realized his other senses were amplified. Every croak, snap or splash sounded like a nearby monster, although whatever made the grunting noises probably really was a monster. After a while they decided whatever had grunted was not coming up after them, and they agreed to try to get some sleep. It eluded Bill though as he listened to the sounds of the night. He doubted Robin slept either, but he didn't ask.

They yawned in greeting to the morning. Stretching helped work out the kinks they had acquired through the night. Although the sky was clear, everything was still wet, so they decided not to even attempt a fire. Again, their meal consisted of protein bars.

As they brought their gear down to the raft, Bill spotted streaks in the mud not far away which looked like a big stick had been drawn across the flat. "What would make that type of mark?"

"Gator," Robin replied. "And by the width of those marks, I'd say a pretty big one. Like the one that got Captain Hook." Or the man at the plane from the first day.

Bill kept a close eye on the water as they loaded the rest of their gear. They took turns relieving themselves and then pushed off. Initially, they had energy, and they reached the mouth of the St. Croix River within two hours. They were surprised by the size of the St. Croix. It was larger than the Mississippi, a detail strikingly different from their old world.

As the morning wore on, they began to feel lethargic due to their lack of sleep. They continued to make progress but much more from the current carrying them along than from their own paddling. Luckily, the current was stronger once they passed the St. Croix.

A little before noon, they put ashore at the head of a small island and made a fire from gathered sticks and dead branches. They heated up a couple of cans of soup. Robin commented on how they did it backwards. They should have had the soup the previous evening when they were all wet and cold and, instead, saved the protein bars, beef jerky and apples for lunch. But they were tired of the protein bars. After they cleaned out the pot with river water and stowed it away, they climbed the high sandy bank and lay back.

They watched a few billowy clouds drift along in the baby blue sky. Bill noticed Robin had fallen asleep. Better to let her get some rest he thought. He thought about his mom. He missed her. He thought about those gator noises from the previous night. He was tired and closed his eyes for a moment to rest.

Bill could sense that he was being stalked, but nothing was quite real. Sort of fuzzy. He had to get to a safer place, but he wasn't sure where that was, so he ran. He noticed Robin was with him and they ran through the woods together. He held her hand. He heard branches crack behind him, but he didn't have time to look. He didn't dare. He wanted to know what was behind him, but he also didn't want to know because all he wanted to do was escape. He just ran and ran and dragged Robin with him. She tripped and fell to the ground. He had to get her up, but she was stuck. Robin screamed at him to run, but he was paralyzed. How could he just leave her there for the monsters? Then the raptors came at them from three sides. But these raptors were huge like rexes. How could they be so big and yet so fast? He felt helpless. He couldn't help Robin or himself. He heard the roar of a rex and then realized he was in a dream.

Bill opened his eyes, still troubled by his nightmare. Robin's eyes were open too, and she had her head turned toward him. Their eyes connected, and Bill felt something inside of him. He thought there was a connection. Did Robin feel it too? No, that feeling had to be some residue from the dream.

"Did you hear it too?" she whispered.

He realized where they were and broke out of his reverie. "The roar? Yeah, but I thought I was dreaming," he replied.

"Shush!"

Chapter 20 - Bill

Bill realized the roar which woke him from his nightmare was real. His next thought was for them to get down to the raft and get the heck away from there, but then he realized the noises were from far away. Whatever had just happened was not on their island.

He heard bellowing from up over his head. He and Robin both rolled over onto their bellies and crawled up to the top of a grassy berm above the steep sandy beach. They rose to their knees and peered through the tall grass toward the shore across from the narrow head of the island. Almost straight across from them a small stream flowed gently into the river. Upriver from the stream, a wooded area sloped upward toward a plateau. Downriver of the stream, a few bushes gave way to a flat sandy prairie which stretched for maybe a mile or more to the south.

Two rexes were at the edge of the bushes and faced what looked like a *triceratops*, except it had extra spikes which came off its shield. A few hundred yards to the south were several more of the *triceratops*-like dinosaurs. Somehow, the close one had gotten separated from the herd and bellowed. Was this a warning to the rexes or a call for help from its herd?

"I wonder if that one is sick or injured," Robin said. "Poor guy!"

"So, you think it couldn't keep up with the herd?" Bill asked.

"Probably, and predators prey on the weak and injured as well as the young."

They watched as the huge approaching rexes circled the straggler from opposite sides. They were probably assessing the remaining strength of the lone dinosaur. The horned dinosaur was not small either with a weight nearly as much as one of the rexes. But in a more compact frame and with two long spears attached to a huge shield. It turned toward the rex farthest from the river. That rex stopped, but the other charged in toward the prey. The straggler turned surprisingly fast for its size toward the charging rex. The rex chomped down hard, but it only caught the shield of the dinosaur. As the first rex hung on to the shaking shield, the second rex charged in from the other side and caught the lone dinosaur behind the shield and closed its jaws on the neck.

Even with the distance. Robin and Bill heard the cracking sound as the giant rex broke the animal's neck. Bill couldn't believe the power of those jaws. How much force it must have taken to break the doomed creature's neck.

The animal immediately slumped over. Only its beak-shaped snout moved, trying to capture a few last breaths. The rexes both roared a warning to all other animals in the area to stay away. Then they tore into their prize as each in turn clamped down with gigantic jaws and shook violently. Huge chunks of flesh were torn away and quickly devoured.

"Wow! Wish I could've captured that on video and put it up on YouTube," Bill said.

"You know 'monsters belong in B movies.'"

"What?"

"Just a line from *King Kong*. Never mind. Do you think we will ever get back?" Robin asked.

"I don't know." It was all he could think to say. He looked down at his watch. They had been asleep for about an hour. "We should get back on the river."

"Yeah," she said. "Time to go back to being Tom and Huck."

"More like Charlie and Rose."

"Who?" Robin asked.

"From *The African Queen*. I'd gotten the impression you were good at movie trivia."

"Not the real oldies."

"Hey, look." Bill pointed down to where their raft was pulled up on the beach. Three large fish swam past just a few inches below the surface.

Robin saw them and leaped into action. She ducked low and crept down toward the shore, trying not to spook the fish. As she reached the raft, the fins from the fish still stuck above the water near the shoreline of the island. She grabbed the fishing pole. It had a spoon hook, essentially a shiny slab of metal with a treble hook which dangled off the end, attached to the end of the line. She tossed the lure far past the three fish and reeled it back. The fish ignored it and swam lazily on as the lure flashed past them.

She casted the lure again and, this time, reeled fast as she guided the line over the fish. One of the treble hook barbs buried itself into the side of one of the fish, foul-hooking it.

Bill ran down to her side as soon as he saw the pole bend over. At first, he thought, he should help, but then he remembered how his dad had scolded him for trying to help with a large fish when he was younger. This was between Robin and the fish unless she asked for help.

Robin held onto the rod with both arms and leaned back against the tension as line spun off the reel. The reel buzzed like a bee, and then it started to smoke. Suddenly, it froze up and did not yield line any longer.

Robin was almost pulled into the river with the sudden strong tension, but Bill grabbed around her waist and held on. It seemed they were at a stalemate with the fish until, suddenly, the rod snapped and the whole outfit flew out of her hands into the river in an instant. The fish and the reel were both gone.

"Damn! How could I have been so stupid?" Robin yelled. "That reel was not meant for fish like that. Should have known better than to try something so stupid."

"What were those?" Bill asked.

"Sturgeon. Must have been thirty pounds, easily. Maybe even forty. I bet if I'd a spear instead, I could have gotten one of them," Robin said.

"We have spears," Bill reminded her.

"They're not fish spears. Stab them with one of these, they would slip right off unless you could pin 'em to the bottom. What we need is either tips with barbs on the end or one with multiple tips that splay out when you spear the fish."

Then a roar rolled across the river from behind them. They had almost forgotten about the unfolding drama back there. Time to get back on the water.

At about four in the afternoon, they started evaluating locations for the night. They looked for an island with steep banks like the one they had dozed on earlier. About then, they came to a fork in the river. They couldn't decide which was the main channel since both appeared to be about the same size. Robin pointed out the channels had to come back together again. Therefore, the land between the channels was an island. However, Bill was leery of camping there because they didn't know how big it was. Perhaps, if it were big enough, raptors might roam it.

They continued downriver and knew, if they didn't come upon a better location, they could always go over to the big island. Provided they didn't spot any raptors. Around five, they found a suitable smaller island with banks steep enough they felt comfortably safe from the gators. They estimated the island was well short of a mile long and three hundred yards wide in its middle. They set up camp and got a fire started. They sent a message at six that said "OK. NO REX CHASING US. SOMEWHERE NEAR WHAT WAS REDWING." and finished with the end of message sign.

Bill examined his crimson toes. He had removed his wet shoes and socks in the raft and now realized he had not put lotion on his feet. Bad oversight. It was autumn, but they had been out under the bright sun all day.

Bill heated up a couple more cans of soup and a can of beans while Robin sat down and fashioned herself a fish spear. After they ate, they boiled a pot of river water for them to drink the next day. Once cooled, they poured the water into their used bottles. Maybe a dinosaur or a gator would doom them, but as long as they had fire and the pot, they would not succumb to dehydration.

They slept better than the previous night. A fast current flowed past the head of the island and the steep banks ensured no gator sounds in the night. Bill awoke a few times by thunderous roars of rexes. One of the times, he wondered to himself if those rexes had just announced a kill. But they were all a good distance away, and he easily fell back asleep each time.

They woke for an early start. A heavy blanket of fog covered the river and limited their view to a few hundred yards. The air was cool but not cold as they set out downriver with Robin in the front seat of the raft. A short distance ahead the channel split, and they steered down the larger left side. The channel ahead split again into multiple smaller channels.

Robin stopped with her paddle stuck in mid-air. "Stop! Paddle backwards. No. Go for the shore over to the left. Hurry."

Bill spotted what excited her. Several large dinosaurs stood spanning across the river like a line of giant statues. He hesitated as he stares for a few seconds before paddling hard with Robin to get to the shore of the long island. Once they beached the raft, they grabbed their spears and crept down toward the downriver end of the island.

The island had sandy beaches on both sides, but it was covered with a thick canopy of trees and waist high grass down its center. The island stretched out for about a mile, but most of it was upriver from them. On the other hand, it was narrow, no more than fifty yards at its widest. Another channel flowed past the far side. About a hundred yards down, they came upon a path which cut across in front of them. The grass was flattened and brown.

"What do you suppose made this?" Bill asked.

"Same thing that made those streaks back up at that muddy island. I don't suggest following it. Come on. Keep going."

They continued forward. By the time they reached the tip of the island, the fog had started to rise a little, so visibility was a better than when they had first spotted the dinosaurs. Ahead of them in roughly a line, stood at least nine sailbacks which blocked the river. There could have been more of the beasts farther away, hidden by the fog. The ones they saw all

194 : MJ Konkel

stood in roughly four to five feet of water. Most of the river around them was shallow with only a few deeper channels which cut through at the end of a delta, and ahead was a large lake.

"What are they doing?" Bill asked. "It's like they are forming a blockade against us." Of course, it was absurd to think the dinos were there just for them.

"Yeah, they heard about us coming, probably on their little radios," Robin mocked.

"Not funny." Bill replied.

She stuck out her tongue at him. He frowned, then stuck out his back at her.

"Good thing they're facing downstream," Robin said. "I suspect they are catching fish. Remember those sturgeon we saw yesterday? Bet it's a fall spawning run."

"So how do we get past them?"

"Don't know," Robin replied. "Maybe, we can't. What options do we have? We could turn around and head back to the mall—not my first choice."

"Mine either. It's way too soon to give up. We could go back to the island we were at last night until this run is over," he said.

"That might be a week or more. I don't know about you, but I don't have that type of patience."

He knew he didn't have that much patience either. Besides, they didn't bring enough supplies for such a stay. "What if we wait until it gets dark?"

"Sneak past them at night? We're not going out onto that lake in the dark. I may be crazy, but I'm not stupid."

"Yeah, I didn't like that idea either. Besides, we don't even know if those things can see at night or not," he said.

"In fact, if we are going to do anything, we should do it soon so that we have enough time to get down the lake to where it becomes the river again before nightfall."

"Why?" he asked.

"This is the beginning of Lake Pepin. If it is like the lake on the map, there are no islands on it to stop on for the night." Robin chewed on her lip as she thought for a minute. "The channel on this side of the island seems to have a deeper center, and there's a gap between those two sailbacks." She pointed at two particularly large ones. Had to be the biggest ones.

Bill stared where she pointed. It appeared the two dinosaurs were about a hundred yards apart. "You're not suggesting going right by between them. Are you? That's just as crazy as going at night. Maybe crazier."

"I don't think it's as crazy as it first seems," she said. "They are facing the other direction, so they're not likely to see us coming down the river. The current is swift past those sand bars. We zip past them quickly and get out into that deeper water before they even spot us."

"And if they come after us?"

"I think they're too concentrated on the fish. It's like when bears are fishing for salmon."

Bill groaned. "I don't know." He felt uncomfortable about it but felt he didn't want Robin to think he was a coward. "All right, but if we're going to do this, we better get at it. And if I get killed, I'm blaming you."

On the trip back up to the raft, they followed their path of trampled grass they had made on their way down. The fog continued to lift. Bill wished it had stayed to make them less visible as they approached the sailbacks. Suddenly Robin stopped and put her hand out.

"What is it?" Bill's eyes glanced around and searched for danger. "Is it the gator that made that trail?"

"No. Over there. It's a fish," she answered.

"Christ! You scared me there. Thought it was the gator or maybe even a sailback ahead of us. Let's keep going."

"No. I'm going to get it with my new spear."

"Let it be. We don't have time for fishing," Bill said.

"This trip is taking longer than we planned. At least an extra day. Not to mention, what happens if there is no one there? This won't take long. Looks like the fish was injured. Probably escaped from one of those sailbacks. It'll be easy."

The fact that she said it would be "easy" made him uncomfortable. It sounded too much like famous last words. "The fog's lifting. We'd better get going before it's totally gone," he said.

"It's already too far gone to be of any use as a cover. I'm also thinking this fish might be useful. Think of it as something we could use as a bribe."

"A bribe?" he asked.

"Yeah, or a diversion. If it looks like one of those sailbacks is really coming after us, we toss the fish to it and make our getaway while it's eating."

"Doubt it will buy us much of a head start. That fish would only be a small snack for those monsters."

"They're feeding on them now, and it might be all we need to distract one of them until we get past it."

Bill didn't say anything further. He conceded, but he wasn't happy with the delay. Robin crouched down to give herself a low profile and slowly inched forward through the grass until she was right at the edge of the bank. Bill had difficulty seeing the fish from his vantage point, but he watched Robin inch even closer to the bank. He peered around, making sure no dinosaurs were around. She suddenly thrusted her spear downward.

There were loud splashes as the fish tried to escape, and Robin leaped off the bank. She fought with it, so he leaped over the bank to help. He tried to get his hand under its fat belly to lift it, but the tail thrashed vigorously from side to side and prevented a good grip. He changed tactics. He clutched the tail and felt its powerful muscles as it struggled to wriggle free. But he held on and helped Robin haul it ashore.

"It's a sturgeon," Robin said.

Bill eyeballed it. "It has to be at least fifteen pounds."

"Fifteen? Try more like twenty, easily." Robin struggled to get her fish spear out of the sturgeon's head. "Maybe even 25 pounds."

Bill could see this was a fish story that was going to grow in the future, assuming they had a future. The fish continued to thrash to free itself, but it was losing energy. He grabbed it under the gill flap and dragged it along as they hurried back to the raft. He wondered where they would store the catch until they had time to cook and eat it. He also wondered if it might bring trouble instead.

Chapter 21 - DeJuan

The herd of duck bills, just east of the mall, munched on tall brown grass which had grown to over five feet tall beyond the mall zone. DeJuan watched them with wishful eyes. Their fresh meat from the mall was now gone. It seemed like such a shame so much of it had to be thrown out.

"What I wouldn't give for my old M82 right now," Joel said. They had the handguns and a handful of ammo, but they were saving it for defense. Besides, they would have to be mighty lucky to drop a hadrosaur with those.

"M82? What's that?" DeJuan asked.

"Just a rifle," Joel replied.

"Changing the subject," DeJuan said, "I've been thinking about those gangsters' cars. We should go back."

"What for?" Joel asked.

"We think there were four of them guys in those cars, but we only recovered two guns. Perhaps there is another gun or two. We didn't look under the seats or in the trunks."

"You're forgetting about that rex that keeps appearing over in that vicinity."

"I'm thinking he has moved out. Gone south for the winter. Besides, I have an idea for distracting them, even if there is another one there to replace him."

Joel squinted at DeJuan. "You're really serious about going back there."

"Yeah. You in?"

"I think you're crazy."

Nevertheless, an hour later Joel was with DeJuan as they and a few others had talked into coming crouched behind the trees just west of Ikea's parking lot.

"I think your whim to come out here was out of boredom," Joel said.

"And you?" DeJuan asked.

Joel chuckled. "A boy needs a hobby."

"I'm think you're both freaking nuts," An Dung said. "I'm probably just as nuts as well for letting myself be talked into this crazy scheme."

L'Troy remained silent. He kept his eyeballs glued to the woods ahead of them rather than be distracted by the banter.

"Well, I don't see anything out there," An Dung said. "It's been like half an hour we've been sitting here doing nothing."

"Joel?" DeJuan trusted Joel's instincts more than his own for this kind of thing.

"I haven't seen anything either," Joel said. "Let's go forward but keep alert. Those rexes seem able to sneak up on us."

The foursome left the cover of the trees. Up until then, if they had seen a rex they could have easily dashed under the parking structure of Ikea where only a juvenile rex would be able to follow. As they moved forward, their chances of outrunning a rex decreased.

"Sky is much different than the last time we were here. Remember the rain?" DeJuan asked.

"Dude, you're talking about the weather," An Dung said.

DeJuan realized he had yapped because he was nervous. He shut his mouth and peered deeper into the woods ahead of them.

Suddenly they heard branches break at the edge of the tree line off to their right. They raised their spears in response. If it were a raptor or group of raptors, they would stay and fight with their guns and their spears, if necessary. There wasn't a chance they could outrun raptors. If it were a rex, they would have no choice but to run.

A trio of duck bills stepped out into the open. DeJuan and the others lowered their spears as the three trotted across the open space just to the north of Ikea, stopped and munched on the tall grass which was still green there.

DeJuan followed as Joel crept across toward the cars. Joel reached the Cadillac first and found the trunk release. DeJuan and L'Troy rummaged through the trunk while Joel looked inside the interior which was no longer the interior because a rex had ripped off the roof.

"I got nothing useful up here," Joel said in a low voice. "You guys find anything useful in the trunk?"

The car was on its side, so most of what was in the trunk had all piled up on the one side. "Do four boxes of condoms count as useful?" L'Troy asked.

"That was one confident dude," An Dung said. He kept his gaze on the woods while the others searched.

"Or hopeful," L'Troy said. He took several steps deeper into the woods and looked up into a tree. He caught DeJuan's attention and pointed up at the boat still caught in the branches. "What about that?"

DeJuan peered up. "Go for it."

L'Troy jumped, caught a branch, and started climbing up into the tree.

Meanwhile, Joel found the trunk release for the Impala, and DeJuan rummaged through the trunk. He lifted a pile of old musty blankets.

"Joel, I got something for you," DeJuan whispered.

Joel stepped around and climbed over the tree trunk which held up the back end of the car. DeJuan handed over a shotgun.

"Twelve-gauge. Awe, an early Christmas present." Joel held the gun and looked at it. The gray gunmetal shined like it was new. The wood on the stock and the pump also appeared brand new.

DeJuan turned his gaze from the gun to Joel. "Christmas isn't until December 25th. The number of days left until—"

"Just a figure of speech, DeJuan."

"Oh! Of course." DeJuan returned to rummaging in the trunk but kept an eye on the shotgun.

Joel pulled down on the pump of the gun, and it spat out a shell out of the chamber. Two more pumps, and two more shells flew out. He turned the gun sideways and peered into the empty chamber. Picking up the shells, he placed one back into the chamber and one into magazine loading port. He held up and examined the third shell before sliding it into the magazine as well. "Buckshot, size 0."

"Whole box of shells in here too." DeJuan pulled the box out of the trunk and opened it. "Says 25 on the outside, but it appears to be missing three."

Joel picked out a shell from the box and tried to stuff it into the magazine, but he was only able to push the shell halfway inside. "Mm. These guys bought one designed for bird hunting. Limits it to two in the magazine and one in the chamber. They could easily have modified it to hold two more. I'll do that once we're back at the mall."

"Guys," An Dung whispered, "I just saw movement out there."

Joel and DeJuan froze except for their eyeballs. Their heads turned toward the woods.

"Where?" Joel whispered.

"Tree branches swaying over there." An Dung pointed deep into the trees.

The three of them watched but dared not move. Everything was eerily silent. Then a big branch slowly bent, and behind it towered a rex still most hidden by the foliage. It took a step in their direction and was only about forty yards away. The beast was a big one. Not as big as the one from before, but more than big enough to qualify as the new king of the land.

The three of them slowly crept backwards and crouched behind the Impala. L'Troy remained stuck in the tree.

"Hope your idea works because I don't know if this is going to even slow him down." Joel gently patted the shotgun in his hands.

"Me too." DeJuan pulled a controller out of his backpack. He peered up over the hood and watched the rex take two more steps in their direction. Each enormous stride covered more than three yards but made very little noise.

DeJuan flipped the power switch on and pushed the throttle knob on his controls. They immediately heard the buzzing sound of the drone as it took off into the air from behind them. Yard to two-yard-long strands of crepe paper hung from the drone as DeJuan steered it over them and toward the rex.

The drone then took a sharp left turn and buzzed parallel to the highway. DeJuan used the screen on the controls to see where the drone flew, but he visually watched the rex at the same time. The rex took the bait and chased after the drone. DeJuan had to fly it fast enough to stay ahead of the rex, but not so fast the rex gave up on it, all while avoiding flying the drone into something. The rex seemed attracted by the drone's bright red tails. The rex lunged once with its jaws and got a tad of paper which tore away. Soon the rex and the drone were out of sight, and DeJuan relied instead on the drone's camera to both know the rex's position as well as a path toward where it led the rex. Soon the rex was a few hundred yards away.

"We have a problem!" L'Troy yelled. He was still up in the tree, and he pointed out deeper into the woods. "A big problem!"

DeJuan turned and saw another rex standing about fifty yards away just to the right of where the first one had first appeared.

"No problem," DeJuan said. "I'll just fly the drone up into the sky and bring it back here." He played with the controls' knobs, but it didn't go like he planned. "Uh oh!"

"Uh oh?" An Dung stared at DeJuan.

"Drone's caught in some branches."

The second rex lumbered toward them. "Get under," DeJuan said. An Dung crawled under the Impala and back up against the log. Joel stood crouched behind the car and waited with his new shotgun.

"What are you doing?" DeJuan whispered from a knee. "We gotta get under the car."

"If he turns the right way, I going to pop his eye," Joel whispered.

DeJuan raised his head and peered over the top of the back of the sedan. The rex stopped fifteen yards away and tilted its head upward. Why hadn't Joel fired at it yet? Perhaps he didn't have the shot he wanted yet.

The rex lifted itself from a horizontal stance to a more upright stance, and its snout continued upward until it just grazed the bottom of the boat. It snorted. Then it banged the bottom of the boat with the very tip of its snout. L'Troy had hid himself inside the boat, but the rex had sniffed him out. It couldn't quite reach him.

It was close enough for L'Troy though. He scrambled out and reached for a higher branch. L'Troy held onto something. A flare gun he had found in the boat. He struggled to grab the next branch. Shaking, he pointed the gun at the rex and started to pull the trigger, but then he lost his balance. He grabbed onto a nearby branch and caught himself from falling. But the flare sailed way high over the head of the rex. Not even close.

The rex took a step forward and then shifted its head so it was directly below L'Troy. It spread its jaws wide and gave out a deafening roar upward right into the L'Troy's face. The flare gun dropped and fell straight into the open jaws of the rex. L'Troy wrapped his arms tight around the thick branch and squeezed his eyes shut. The rex peered at L'Troy for a moment and then spread his jaws wide again up another roar, but it cut short. It snapped its jaws shut and pivoted its head toward the direction where the other rex had disappeared.

"Oh, no!" DeJuan said. "First one must be coming back."

But the second rex turned in the opposite direction and fled.

"DeJuan, An Dung, get out the hell out of here. Everybody, move," Joel yelled.

DeJuan scrambled to his feet. "What's going on?"

"It's not the rex." Joel pointed in the direction the flare had been sent. A fire had quickly sprung up and grew. It spread in all directions, including back toward them. He turned toward the tree. "L'Troy, you have to get down now."

L'Troy did not move other than he visibly shook as he clung tight to the branch.

"Move it now or die," Joel shouted.

L'Troy craned his neck and peered down at them. He then climbed slowly down branch by branch. They watched as the fire jumped between trees, lighting up new ones as the flames spread. Finally L'Troy fell from the last branch onto the ground and rolled. He stumbled to his feet and followed the others as they dashed to the Ikea parking lot where they stopped and turned to stare at the growing blaze.

All sorts of dinosaurs, from duck bills to raptors, emerged from the woods and stampeded out into the open space. DeJuan and the others found shelter under the parking ramp as the animals stampeded past. So many that DeJuan quickly lost count. Some species passed by which they had not even seen before.

L'Troy put his hands on his hips as he tried to catch his breath. "Thought I was going to pass out up there. When that rex roared in my face, I started to freaking black out."

"Dude, you would have fallen right into its open jaws," An Dung said.

"Yeah, I know. All I could freaking do was grab that branch and wrap myself around it. Was like it was screwing with my head. Like I lost track of what's up and what's down."

"Vertigo," DeJuan said.

"Yeah, that shit," L'Troy said.

"Can't believe Robin ever suggested we start hunting these monsters," DeJuan said.

"I didn't hear you telling her it was crazy," An Dung said.

"Well, maybe not the rexes, but we are going to start needing meat from somewhere," Joel said.

They watched as the blaze quickly spread to the north of them and wrapped around, fueled by a modest breeze which came from the southwest. They felt the intense heat given off from the inferno, even at their distance from it. One tree after another just burst into flame and toppled over. All the animals that made it out were well past them by then, and they thought it was best to return to the mall as the giant fire continued to spread toward the east.

"Way that fire spread so fast," DeJuan said, "it's almost like the woods has extra oxygen fueling the flames." But that seemed implausible. He turned his thoughts elsewhere. DeJuan thought about his latest adventure as another he would someday tell his future children. Assuming he ever had any. Assuming he managed to live long enough. Oh well, they would never believe the stories anyway.

Chapter 22 - Bill

Bill glanced over his shoulder. He had not heard or seen anything nor had any reason to suspect anything lurked behind them. It was just a habit he had started to acquire, a valuable habit in a world inhabited by carnivorous dinosaurs.

Ahead of them, the sailbacks were spread out across the shallow sand bars of the river. He glanced at each of the five closest ones. Thank goodness, they all seemed to be focused downriver.

The raft floated rapidly along, kept to the center of the channel as he steered with the rudder. He and Robin held their paddles motionless but ready. The sturgeon trailed behind, tethered to the raft by a thin rope tied in a loop through its mouth and out one of its gill flaps. If they needed, they could quickly fling the fish with the rope. They had ditched the cooler and set the remaining water bottles on the raft.

The plan was to quietly float until either they were just passing through between the two closest sailbacks or one of the sailbacks started to move toward them. They were within a hundred yards of the line formed by the sailbacks, and none had yet taken notice of their raft. Close overhead, pterodactyls circled like vultures. All the sailbacks stood on four legs as seemed typical of them, although Bill had seen the beasts rise onto their hind legs before.

Fifty yards to the line separating the two closest sailbacks. Still, none of them had seemed to have even noticed the raft. Then the sailback on the right craned its snout and stared their direction. Bill felt the hairs on his arms stand up, and he was ready to attack the river with his paddle.

But the sailback only stared at them, not moving, from fifty yards away. Then Bill saw, in his peripheral vision, the one on their left suddenly shoot its head forward into the river. Adrenaline kicked in.

"Go! Go! Go!" he shouted. His paddle dug in, and he moved like a madman. Robin joined him.

The sailback's head came back up with a large fish, another sturgeon, caught crosswise in its narrow toothy jaws. It threw the fish farther back into its jaw with a little head toss and chomped down. The fish's tail dropped into the river. The fish's head dangled from the side of the sailback's jaw by a piece of skin until the sailback chomped down again, and the head dropped as well. The sailback eased the remainder of the fish down its gullet. Then it rushed forward and found the head it had dropped while the tail floated away.

Bill continuously looked back over his shoulder as he paddled, although he paddled slower as fatigue set in and since none of the dinosaurs had actually come

212 : MJ Konkel

after them. "It appears the sailbacks don't like to swim."

"Maybe, but some had to have swum to get to some of those sandbars," Robin said.

Bill paddled faster again. He watched as a pair of pterodactyls swooped down. One beat out the other and scooped up the sailback's lost fish tail with its long, pointed beak. The flying reptile then banked and flapped its long, thin wings to gain more altitude and get away from its rival.

"I think it's safe to slow down and breathe again." Robin laid her paddle across her lap.

"Christ! That was scary back there." Bill stopped paddling as well. "But again, wish I had a video of that and could put it up on YouTube."

"You could write a book," Robin said.

"A book?" Bill thought about it for a few seconds. "Got a title. Bill's Thrills with Dinosaurs."

"Or maybe, Why I Shit My Pants a Hundred Times."

"Come on! Tell me that didn't scare you too."

Robin shrugged. "Wasn't scared."

"Either you're lying your ass off, or there's something wrong with you," Bill said.

"Okay, maybe it was a little scary."

"A little scary?" Bill asked.

Robin let out a little chuckle. "Scary enough to shit my pants."

"Do you mean—"

"Figure of speech, Bill." She put her paddle back into the water. "We better get going. We have eight, nine, maybe even ten hours of paddling before we can stop for the night. On the lake here, we won't have the luxury of the current pulling us along. If we're lucky, the wind'll be at our backs."

They paddled for a while, keeping an easy but steady pace. About an hour after they left the sailbacks behind them, something tugged on the rope which held their fish. Bill reeled the rope in hand over hand; all that was left was a head.

About the same time, a head popped up above the lake a short distance from them. It startled them. Bill and Robin both dropped their paddles on the raft and reached for their spears. The creature swam in a big circle around them but did not approach the raft.

The water was clearer in the lake than the river behind them, and they saw the body of the creature. It looked like a miniature version of the Loch Ness monster with a long slender neck, a slightly flattened-out American football-shaped body and four large flippers. Unlike the supposed Loch Ness monster, the tail was rather short. This version probably only weighed about a hundred pounds.

Then a second head identical to the first popped up out of the lake. The creatures did not come closer but just seemed to watch them on the raft.

After ten minutes Bill tore the head of the fish off the rope and tossed it at one of the creatures. The creature dove under the surface and come up under the fish head. A few seconds later the second creature was at the fish head too. They took turns and bit out chunks from it. When it was devoured, the second

214 : MJ Konkel

creature disappeared. The first one rolled over onto its back and whacked its front flippers twice together before it performed a reverse dive down into the lake and disappeared.

"That was weird," Robin said. "It was like it was applauding us. Well, I'm not standing up to take a bow."

"It did sort of look like that's what it was doing, didn't it?" Bill said. "But I'd bet that was just some type of natural behavior for them."

"Yeah. Probably their way of giving us the finger."

"They seemed friendly to me," Bill said. "Almost like porpoises."

Robin's face had a scowl. "They're no porpoises. They stole our fish, the little monsters!"

"They looked like little Loch Ness monsters," Bill said.

"Fish-stealing Loch Pepin monsters," Robin said, "You shouldn't have given them the head. They didn't deserve it."

Bill thought she clearly was not going to let it go that her prize fish was taken. "We should get moving. Sun's starting to climb."

The lake was about two miles wide but stretched out many miles long. It really was just a widening of the river to the point where a current was not readily noticeable. The western shore was a huge sand bar, and they followed offshore from it. Sometimes, one would stop to rest for a few minutes while the other continued to paddle. The openness of the bar ensured that they wouldn't be surprised by carnivores and gave them a place to safely beach the raft occasionally to relieve themselves and stretch their legs. The bar would provide no protection if they had to stay through the night on it though. They discussed this and decided that if it became dark before they came to an island, they would anchor out in the middle of the lake for the night.

They saw more of the triceratops-like dinosaurs. They discussed what to call them and settled on toppers due to the resemblance to *triceratops* although Robin had initially lobbied for lotsatops.

In early afternoon, Bill and Robin stopped on another long sandy beach and again stretched their legs and relieved themselves. After that the terrain adjacent to the lake changed to woods, and the slope became steeper and rockier near the shore as the hills closed in. As the afternoon wore on, it became obvious they would not find more places they could safely stop on the western side of the lake. It appeared the large open sandbars were now on the opposite side of the lake. That would take an extra 45 minutes if they decided to cross, and their arms were already sore. Instead, they continued down the western shore.

It was another two and a half hours before they reached the end of the lake. The eastern shoreline curved and came out straight at them as a huge sandbar that blocked off the eastern side. That was what had backed up the river and created the lake they were exiting. The sandbar had been built by the Chippewa River just below which dumped sand continuously as its current slackened once it met the Mississippi.

It was another hour before they came to an island where they could stop, and it was well past five by then. The large crescent-shaped island mirrored a curve in the river and had a steep bank as they approached. A strong current pulled where they put ashore. They had to tie the raft to a fallen tree and pull themselves up the bank. As soon as they climbed the bank, they discovered the inside curve of the island was flatter and harbored a current-free slough. It had the appearance of an area that could be home to gators. It was late, though, and they had no time to look for a better spot.

They worked quickly to get their message sent back to the mall by six. They had no desire to be on the ground for the night, so they hung up the ultralight hammocks between the trees well above the ground and slept in sleeping bags. Later Bill lay back under the stars for what turned out to be a clear crisp night. Although he heard a lot of loud splashes, he did not hear grunts or the sounds of cracking sticks from the woods of their island, and he soon nodded off and slept soundly.

Chapter 23 - Robin

Robin woke before Bill. The sky became light as the sun peeked up over the hills toward the east. Robin was still irked by the theft of her fish. It could have saved them a day's rations. Yes, there was more meat on one side of it than they could have eaten in a day, and they would not have stopped to take the time to smoke it, but those thieves didn't have to steal the whole fish. Water under the bridge. Maybe she could get another one and grill it for breakfast. Maybe even before Bill got up out of his sleeping bag. He tended to sleep longer than her.

She looked down by the raft. The high bank gave her a good vantage point to stare down on the fast-flowing river, but she could not spot anything in the water in the fifteen minutes she searched. She decided to explore over on the other side of the narrow island. Bill was awake by then, so she let him know what she planned. So much for surprising him. As much as she picked on him, she was more than a little fond of the big galoot.

The west side, protected by the curvature of the island, was calm with no current until far out into the channel. Near the island, the river was shallow, and the slope up onto the bank was gentle and sandy. A school of small fish burst from the surface just a short distance from her. That encouraged her. Something chased those small fish. Probably a bigger fish. She edged down closer to where she saw the activity and very slowly waded out until she was knee deep. There she waited.

There was nothing to do but watch the water. Her mind wondered. She thought about all that had happened. She realized her thoughts continuously returned to Bill. She observed other small fish and minnows bursting out of the water, but not close to her.

Then she saw a wake approach toward her. It came almost straight at her but veered away at the last second. She plunged her spear down into the front of the wake and felt her spear yanked back and forth. Robin lifted the spear out of the water, and a fish dangled off the end of it. She waded toward the shore, proud of herself. She had speared a good one. It was a catfish, about three pounds, with a large flat head and a brown body. Her dad had always called these mudcats, but she had heard others call them flatheads or yellow cats.

She was startled by a loud clapping noise, but it was only Bill who applauded her catch. "Bravo! Bravo! Heard the splashing and figured either you got something, or something got you."

"It's a big one. Five, maybe even six pounds." She proudly held it up for him to see as she walked toward him.

Then both of their heads turned toward where they heard splashes and saw motion out of the corners of their eyes. Across the channel from them, no more than a hundred yards away, a sailback waded into the river and appeared to head toward them. It was smaller than the ones they saw upriver, maybe a thousand pounds at the most. Just a juvenile but still a monster.

"Run!" Bill yelled.

"To the raft. Leave everything you can't grab as you run," Robin yelled.

The sailback swam slowly as its undulating tail propelled it through the water toward them. They reached the point where they were about to cut across the island toward the raft, but then enormous splashing sounds and loud high-pitched shrieks filled the air. Robin peeked over her shoulders.

The sailback thrashed and rolled on the surface and then down under, and a gigantic gator rolled on top with its jaws locked onto one of the sailback's front legs. Robin stopped to stare at the spectacle. "Turn around and look," she yelled.

Bill turned and his jaw dropped. "My lord, that's a monster of a gator."

"Can't believe it. He's got that sailback in a death roll," Robin said. "Unless it can pull free, it'll drown."

"And the gator can stay under?" Bill asked.

"Yeah, I'd bet at least twenty minutes. I'm sure the sailback can't hold its breath that long. We haven't seen sailbacks swim before. They must have to from time to time like back up there at those sandbars." She pointed back upriver. "I don't think they like to do it, and I think we now know why. " When they stand in shallow water, the sailbacks prey on the gators. But if they go out into deeper water, the big gators prey on them.

"Go gator! *Thank you*, Tic Toc," Bill shouted.

"The crocodile from *Peter Pan*."

"You're good with movie trivia. Why didn't you ever play our game with us?"

"Always more fun to just listen."

Bill stared back at the river which was now calm except for ripples from the attack which continued to spread out. "Do you think a gator like that would attack our raft?"

"Can't say for sure, but probably. Long as we stick to the main channel, I think we'll be pretty safe though."

"Man, there're so freaking many creatures that want to eat us on this world," Bill said.

"I hear you, but they haven't eaten us yet." She put her hand on his back. Then as she realized where her hand was, she pulled it away.

The rolling had stopped, and nothing reappeared above the surface. "Let's get out of here," Bill said.

Thanks to the gator, they had plenty of time to pack up their gear before they headed downriver with their raft. Robin put her trophy fish on the deck of the raft, not trusting the thieving Loch Pepin monsters anymore.

After an hour they stopped at a small island and built a fire over which to cook the fish. It wasn't the best tasting fish they had ever eaten, but it filled their bellies and gave them energy for the day. And it allowed them to conserve some rations in case they had to paddle back to the mall.

The rest of the day and the following one were rather uneventful for the two. They made steady progress as they paddled downriver and the river itself assisted them along with it. The river meandered between the high hills which contained it. Occasionally, small tributaries added to the flow. The river often ran through several channels with large islands between them. Sometimes, it was impossible to say which was the main channel, but all channels eventually came back together.

The morning of the fifth day on the river was a complete washout. While the precipitation was not heavy, the strong winds made travel too hazardous. Steady winds from the northwest created whitecaps on the more wide-open stretches of the river. Robin hunkered down with Bill in their tent, and they waited it out.

By the middle of the day, the rain had largely subsided, and the wind had decreased in ferocity. They tired of being cooped and poked their heads out of the tent. Large waves still rolled down the open stretches in the middle of the river, but they figured they would be safe so long as they stuck close to the shores of the islands, partially protected from the wind.

They packed their gear and casted off downriver. Although the wind blew them toward the shorelines of the islands, the waves were manageable. Robin and Bill continuously pushed off away from the shore and away from fallen trees in the river which could damage the floats on their raft. They made progress, but the constant battle with the wind was exhausting.

Around four in the afternoon, they discussed whether it was time to pull over for the night at the island on their left. It had nice high sandy beaches and plenty of deadfall for a fire.

"Hey look! Is that …" Robin shouted. "It is. There's a house up on that hillside."

Chapter 24 - Bill

Where?" Bill squinted to see where Robin pointed. "It is a house."

"Thanks for the vote of confidence that I might possibly know what a house looks like."

"That was snide," Bill growled. He sighed. "We should try to get to it. Maybe, there's someone still there."

"Sorry." Robin gazed out over the wide river between them and the hillside. "It's way too windy to try to cross the main channel right now. We could set up camp right here for the night, but I think we should go a little farther. I want to see what is around the bend."

Bill couldn't believe what he just heard. The "S" word came from her lips. He never heard her say it to anyone much less him before. He had more important things to focus on at the moment, though, so he didn't dwell on it for more than a moment.

"This means DeJuan was right. The Brown's Station people must be here," Robin said.

"Or at least they were."

They followed close to the island as the river hooked to the left. A dam appeared ahead of them. As they continued, they saw more and more of the dam until it and the adjacent spillway system were fully visible. But they had come to the end of the island they had stuck close to for protection from the waves.

"What do we do?" Robin asked. "If we go all the way to the dam today, it'll be after well after five by then. It'll be almost dark by then."

Bill glanced up at the sun. "Yeah, it does get dark sooner down here in the valley, but there might be people over there."

"What worries me is the wind is still pretty stiff, and that open stretch still has some pretty big waves." Robin stared at the open water between the end of the island and the lock and dam. "Our raft was not built for that."

"What if we just keep the raft pointed so our back is to the wind. The wind will take us into the rocks to the left of the dam. That also would keep us in the lee of this island and the waves are not quite as big through there."

Bill watched Robin chew on her lip as she thought about it. The more he thought about it, the more scared he became of that open stretch. Maybe crossing it then wasn't such a good idea after all, and they should just go over to the island for the night. Cross in the morning.

"All right," Robin said.

"All right?" He was no longer sure but felt he had committed to the plan since he had suggested it. "All right, we cross. But we have to keep it straight, or we might get overturned. And we should get going right away, so we can get across before it gets dark."

"Start paddling then," Robin said.

Bill saw excitement in her because there might be people over there. He worried what Robin would think of him if he changed his mind. But he was even more worried about the crossing and whether it was a smart decision.

"Bill." She got his attention. "If we die, I'm blaming you."

Bill smiled as he put his already aching shoulder muscles into his share of powering them across the stretch. The smile quickly disappeared when he thought if she died on this crossing, he would really be to blame.

Waves lapped hard into and over the back of the raft and drenched them with a repetitive spray. Bill got especially soaked as he sat on the back seat. With the wind at their backs though, they quickly sailed across the gap.

They had crossed most of the open stretch of water when a sudden rogue wind gust caught them crosswise and started to turn them sideways to the waves. Before they could straighten the raft back out, a large wave caught them and turned them to angle even more sideways to the waves after it passed.

Bill vigorously paddled to straighten the raft back out. But then another particularly large wave caught them, and they both went over the side of the raft and into the river.

Bill fought his way back to the surface and immediately searched for Robin. His ears filled with the roar of the river being squeezed through the roller gates of the dam downstream from him. Waves lapped over him. Where was Robin? It was impossible to see any distance because of the waves. If she drowned, it would be his fault, and he would have to live with it the rest of his life. However short the rest of his life may be.

"Robin?" he shouted. "Robin! Where are you?"

Chapter 25 - DeJuan

P ancakes again." DeJuan joined the table with
Joel, L'Troy, An Dung, Camila, Alanna, and
Father O'Brien for breakfast.

"What I wouldn't give for a steak and egg
breakfast," L'Troy said.

"Or even some real cream for the coffee," DeJuan
said. "Don't get me wrong. I think this is great coffee,
but I like real cream in mine. Not this powdery stuff."

"The view sure has changed," Alanna stared out
toward the east. The woodland was now ashes and
charred logs all the way up to where the Mississippi
and Minnesota Rivers met. To the east, woodland still
stood.

"You can thank L'Troy for that," An Dung said.
"He shot the flare."

"What would you have done if that monster was
inches from your butt?" L'Troy said.

"It was more than a few inches from you," An
Dung said.

L'Troy's nostrils flared. "I could smell its damn
breath."

DeJuan caught Joel staring at An Dung. Was Joel signaling An Dung to back off? DeJuan had problems interpreting such signals, but he thought he was getting better at it. It was a good time to steer the tone of the conversation. "The fire might not have been such a bad thing."

"How so?" Alanna asked.

"It pushed most of the dangerous rexes and other dinos away from here."

"It opened up the space so we can see farther too," Joel added. "When we go back over to Ikea for supplies we'll be better able to see if there is a rex or raptors waiting to ambush us."

"Not to mention going to one of the rivers, like when Bill and Robin went," DeJuan said. He wondered how they fared. The table got quiet.

L'Troy broke the silence. "Does everyone remember when Robin suggested we go hunt down a dino?"

"Yeah," DeJuan replied, "what about it?"

"Just thinking I would prefer a steak." L'Troy poked his fork at the syrup-soaked pancake on his plate. "Well, guess I should be grateful for the food we have."

"Maybe we should consider how we could do it," Joel said.

Alanna squinted at Joel. "You, of all people, should know how dangerous those monsters are."

"I think that is the craziest thing I ever heard," Camila added. "Es totalmente loco!"

"I'm not suggesting we go out there with spears or even guns and hunt them down," Joel said. "I was thinking more in the lines of some type of trap. Lure them in with some of the rotten meat we still have around. And set it up close to the mall here so that we can quickly carve it up before another dinosaur comes around."

"How do you propose we get one?" DeJuan asked.

"I hope you not thinking of doing this too?" Camila asked. "Esto es Loco!" She had the habit of reverting to her native tongue whenever she was angry.

DeJuan didn't want to upset Camila, but he did have cravings. "Well, we could use a little more protein in our diets."

"What's wrong with protein bars?" Alanna asked.

"Hate to admit I would prefer a steak," Joel said.

"So would I. Even if it's dinosaur rather than beef." DeJuan stabbed his pancake with his fork as he imagined the pancake was a dinosaur steak.

"Crazy! You two perdió su cordura," Camila shouted.

"Maybe." DeJuan nodded. Maybe they were crazy. But a steak sure sounded pretty good to him. He turned toward Joel. "Are you thinking of the raptorsaurs or something bigger?"

"Anything we can take down."

"I was thinking we could lure one of the rexes into the mall," DeJuan said. "They seemed eager before to come in. But this time we have a huge weight of some sort suspended from up high and we drop it on the critter."

"You want to drop a piano on it?" Father O'Brien chuckled.

"Well, not literally. But, yes, that's the general idea. There are pulleys around that we could use to hoist some really heavy metal object and tie it off until we want it to drop."

"That just might work," Joel said, "but I don't like the idea of purposely leading them into the mall."

"I agree. But I can't think of a good way to get a heavy weight hoisted high enough to take out a rex outside of the mall."

"What about from the parking ramp?" An Dung asked.

"I thought about that, but we would need something so that it wasn't suspended right against the wall. A rex is not going to lean its head up against the wall for us."

"I was thinking of something different," Joel said. "I was imagining a large pit trap with long sharp sticks stuck into the bottom. Covered with camouflage and bait."

"It would still have to be close to the mall," DeJuan said, "since no one is going to want to get caught far from here if a rex comes while we're digging."

"Yes. Close by, but not in the mall," Joel replied. "Maybe, where the hotel used to sit." The south side of the mall.

"Why there?" DeJuan asked.

"If raptorsaurs come to the bait instead, we shoot them from what's left of the second level walkway."

"You've been thinking about this for a while." Alanna stared at Joel.

Joel didn't deny it.

"Trapping a rex is going to require a mighty big hole," An Dung said. "Who's going to dig it?"

"Well, that's where you come in," Joel said.

An Dung didn't laugh. "What if we get five feet down and discover it is nothing but rocks?"

"We dig a test hole first."

"I have another idea," DeJuan said. "How about we extend what's left of the overpass by about twenty feet with something that will break under a rex's weight and put the bait out on the end of that?"

"I'd bet a rex wouldn't go out on a wood platform." L'Troy frowned.

DeJuan said, "We cover it and part of the road with rugs so that it doesn't look any different. And below the ramp we put sharp posts into the ground. Just like with Joel's pit idea."

"It might work," Joel said. "We could leave a trail of bait meat to get them up there."

"It wouldn't be nearly as much work as digging a pit," DeJuan added. "What do you all think?"

Camila stood up. "Es loco." She stomped away.

It was late Tuesday, and DeJuan was almost ready to declare their trap ready and set. He wiped the sweat off his brow with his sleeve and peered through the bright sunshine at the ramp behind him. An Dung had laid the last of the area rugs over the extension held up by braces attached to the guard rails. It held up their weight, but it would easily collapse under an adult rex and maybe even under a juvenile rex, depending on its size. DeJuan examined the rugs and was satisfied with how they nicely overlapped onto the blacktop.

An Dung marched back toward the mall as L'Troy pushed a cart up the Lindau Ramp. About every fifty feet he stopped. He reached into the cart with rubber gloves, pulled out about twenty pounds of paper-wrapped rotten meat, and dropped it onto the road.

DeJuan held his nose pinched shut by the time the cart reached him. "Just put the last of it at the end of the ramp and let's get out of here."

"Surely, you don't expect me to go out there. That can't be freaking safe."

"It's safe all right. An Dung and I have been walking out on that all day and don't call me Shirley." DeJuan didn't watch television, but he did watch movies on occasion. When he got nothing but a blank stare, he exclaimed, "Oh come on! You've never seen *Airplane?*"

"Nope."

"Just get that stinking meat out there. I give you my word it's safe to walk on."

"Why don't you do it then?" L'Troy asked.

"You have the gloves on already."

L'Troy sighed and shook his head. "All right. But if it breaks, and I fall down and die, I'm never speaking to you again."

DeJuan chuckled. "Fair enough."

L'Troy tossed the last of the meat onto the wooden extension, peeled off his gloves, and dropped them into the cart.

Then someone yelled a warning, "Run! A rex is coming!"

They sprinted down the ramp until just where it started to curve down to the Lindau entrance. They froze. A rex stood near where they just built the extension. It had its enormous head cocked upward, and it probably smelled the decaying meat. DeJuan and L'Troy took a few strides farther along the ramp, but the rex stomped their direction.

"The other way!" L'Troy pointed down the highway toward the Killebrew Drive Ramp.

DeJuan gripped L'Troy's arm and pointed. "We can't! Look!" A pack of three raptorsaurs sprinted straight toward what was left of the highway. The raptorsaurs were probably too close to the ramp for them to make it there before the raptorsaurs. Making it to the mall from there would be impossible. The rex stomped toward the ramp which led up to where they stood.

"Crap!" L'Troy cursed. "What do we do now? We're freaking trapped. We're gonna freaking die here."

DeJuan grabbed L'Troy's arm and pushed him. "We're not trapped yet. Back to where the extension begins."

The rex ascended the ramp. It picked up and swallowed each package of the odoriferous meat while swarms of buzzing flies scattered each time.

L'Troy stumbled back to where the cart had been left. He stared at DeJuan "What now?"

"We use that." DeJuan pointed over the end to where he had attached a rolled-up rope ladder.

"Genius!" L'Troy raced over to it and tossed it. It unfurled down to the ground below them. He climbed over the end of the railing, turned around and put one step below the other down the ladder.

DeJuan felt the vibrations of the of the rex's strides through the concrete. The monster came at a leisurely pace, pausing every few strides for a snack. But it kept coming. DeJuan climbed over the rail and started to climb down just above L'Troy.

He heard a low rumbling snort and whipped his head downward. Another rex had moved under them. It reached toward them with wide-open jaws and snapped at them. DeJuan and L'Troy were out of the reach of the jaws, but the rope ladder caught across the giant maw. The rex shook its head violently, and the ropes snapped from the sheer force of the rex's jaws. The remainder of the ladder which still hung from the overpass whipped around as DeJuan and L'Troy held on for their lives.

They bashed hard into the side of the ramp. DeJuan's hand caught between the ladder and the side of the ramp. Pain shot up through his arm. His wrist throbbed. He didn't have time worry about whether it was broken though. He saw L'Troy lose his footing and held on with only his arms. L'Troy's face scrunched with strain.

Then the rex below opened its jaws and gave out a tremendous roar. DeJuan became dizzy. He snaked his good arm around one of the ropes and held tight.

As his vision cleared, he saw L'Troy lose his grip. Fall. As if in slow motion, down into the waiting open jaws of the rex. DeJuan turned away, not able to further watch. He couldn't believe it. L'Troy had just died.

The rex above him took another huge stride, lowered its head, and picked up the last of the meat they had set out. Great! The extension wasn't even long enough to work as a trap. DeJuan chided himself for not having taken into full consideration a large rex's length when they had built the extension. It was his plan. And L'Troy died because of his stupid plan.

Then the rex took another stride forward and the extension gave way as the rex shifted its weight to its front leg. The extension crumbled unevenly, and the rex's legs flailed as it fell. The rex missed the pointed poles they had planted into the ground below the extension which DeJuan had envisioned would pierce through the victim. DeJuan stared down at the fallen behemoth. The fall alone should probably have killed it, but a branch had somehow punctured all the way through its neck.

DeJuan couldn't believe it as the fallen rex thrashed its body against the ground until the branch came out, and the giant scrambled to its feet. Blood flowed out of the wound like water from a fire hose as it staggered in the direction of the Ikea building. It collapsed fifty yards away. They had done it, but at what a terrible cost. Alanna and Camila were right. They were loco when they thought they could hunt rexes.

The second rex strode over toward the fallen one. DeJuan thought at first it was going to eat the fallen one. Instead, it nudged the fallen rex with its snout several times and then gave out a bellowing roar. Rather than leave, it stomped around the fallen one, guarding it.

DeJuan struggled with his good hand and his legs to the top of the ladder and up onto the ramp. He was glad to see the raptorsaurs had disappeared. But L'Troy! Damn it. It was not worth it. He could not get rid of the image of L'Troy falling. It was his fault the man was dead.

A group surrounded DeJuan and Joel at the north side of the mall late in the day; all watched out through the huge glass panes above the entrance. Northwest from them, the rex paced and guarded the fallen rex.

DeJuan stared out at the scene, his hand was all wrapped and hung from a sling. He chastised himself for being such an arrogant bastard.

"It's ruining our chances at getting fresh meat," complained Mr. Wanderluch. "Isn't there any way to scare it off?"

Several people scowled at him, but someone shouted from the back, "We could send out your wife."

Mr. Wanderluch seemed amused until he caught Mrs. Wanderluch staring at him. "Not funny," he mumbled.

"Maybe we can drive a car past it and draw it away," An Dung said.

"What's wrong with you people? We need to forget about the whole idea," Alanna replied. "Enough people have died because of them. We shouldn't be inviting more trouble." Murmurs of approval echoed through the hall. DeJuan noticed Camila was among those who nodded. She was still angry at him.

"Sorta hard to forget about it with that monster still out there," An Dung said. "What could go wrong with driving a car past it to try to lure it away?"

"The car could break down," Camila replied.

"It could work in drawing the rex away," Joel said, "and then the rex returns while we are still cutting it up."

DeJuan realized he nodded in agreement. How could they assure the safety of those out there with the task of slicing up the meat? "If there's nothing else we learned so far, we should have at least learned to respect how dangerous these creatures are."

"We should at least try for L'Troy," An Dung shouted.

Father O'Brien came and put his arm around An Dung's shoulder. An Dung closed his eyes. "He was my friend," he cried. He pulled himself loose from Father O'Brien and ran up the closest escalator.

DeJuan wondered if he or someone should go check on the guy. But he disappeared so fast, DeJuan had no idea where he went.

Someone brought out a box of wine glasses and a couple of bottles. Many of the gathered people filled a glass as they continued to stare out at the two rexes. DeJuan poured an extra glass and brought it to Camila.

He handed it to her and said, "I'm sorry. It was loco to think we could trap one of those."

Camila accepted the glass. "I'm still mad at you." She sounded like she might eventually forgive him though.

Then the screech of car tires filled the air, and everyone stared flabbergasted as a car flew down the ramp to their left and stopped in front of them.

Behind the wheel sat An Dung. He did not look back at everyone staring at him though. His gaze was on the rex. He had stopped at the last place he could before it became the point of no turning back. He could still do a sharp U-turn and safely zip back up the ramp out of reach of the rex, but once he pulled down onto Lindau, his only option would be to race around the mall on the street and stay ahead of the rex.

DeJuan tried to hand his glass to Camila, but it got fumbled in the exchange. It fell into a dead plant; the wine was gone, but the glass was saved by the bush.

DeJuan barely notice as he bolted for the exit, flung the big glass door open with his good arm, and rushed toward An Dung. The windows in the sedan were up, so he tried to open the passenger side door. It was locked. He spun to the back door and jerked its handle. The door popped open, and he dove in.

"An, this is crazy!"

"I have to do this," An Dung said.

"Why?"

"I don't know why. For L'Troy. I don't know. Maybe it's not for L'Troy. Maybe it's for me. I just know I have to try."

"You're gonna get yourself killed."

"If I die, then so be it. But I'm doing it. Now, please, get out and shut the door."

"No." DeJuan glanced at the rex and then back at An Dung.

"Shut the freaking door," An Dung yelled.

"If you must do this, I'm going with you," DeJuan said.

An Dung stared at him for several seconds in the rear-view mirror. "Fine." He returned his gaze forward. "But shut the door."

DeJuan jumped in and yanked the door closed as the car's tires already screeched again. He turned his gaze toward the giant rex which faced them. It opened its jaws, and a loud roar vibrated the car as they accelerated around a turn. DeJuan wondered if the rex was about to charge them.

The rex held its ground though as An Dung steered the car down toward Lindau. They were within thirty yards of the beast; it could no longer continue to ignore them. It charged. The tires squealed as DeJuan felt his body whipped to the left as they turned to the right down Lindau. His head was against the side, and he could no longer see outside. He felt a pain in his wrist as it bumped against the door..

Halfway to the end of the block, DeJuan straightened himself and glanced back over his shoulder through the rear window. "It stopped following us."

An Dung slowed the car to a stop and revved the engine a few times. The rex did not respond, so An Dung put the car in reverse and honked the horn while he watched the rear-view mirror. When they were about thirty yards away, the rex again let out a booming roar and charged at them, clearly agitated.

An Dung yanked the gear shift into drive, but he drove away more slowly than the first time as he attempted to lure the beast away. The rex followed them for a short distance, but then it turned around and trotted back to its fallen mate.

They tried twice more to lure it away, but the rex no longer even budged. It only roared at them from beside the fallen giant. An Dung finally gave up, drove around, and parked under the East Parking Ramp.

"It killed L'Troy," An Dung said. "Why didn't it come after us? Why didn't it come after me?"

DeJuan considered. He could give An Dung a logical answer, but he didn't think it would help. "You believe when L'Troy passed, he went to heaven, right?"

An gave a slow nod.

DeJuan pointed upward. "I think he's looking down on us right now, and you know what I think?"

An Dung slowly shook his head. "What?"

"I think he would be honored we tried."

An Dung seemed to lift his shoulders a little. "I don't know. Maybe."

DeJuan nodded. "Come on. Let me buy you a drink." He gave himself a mental reminder to share with everyone else to keep an extra close eye on An Dung for the next few days.

"All right." An Dung smiled. "The tab's on you, but I got the tip."

The next morning, the rex no longer guarded its fallen mate. It appeared it had concluded its mourning.

Chapter 26 - Bill

The large waves bobbed him up and down like a fishing cork. Made it impossible to see who or what else might be in the river. Where was Robin? He called again for her but got no response.

The raft floated away. Swept by the wind and current. He swam hard toward it. But without their weight on it, the wind pushed it away almost as fast as he could swim. He had not gotten much closer.

"Bill!"

He was sure he heard his name. But from where?

"Let it go! You got to swim to the shore. Now!" There she was. She had reached the rocks next to the dam.

In an instant, he realized why she screamed. His heart pounded. He screamed too.

He reached out stroke after stroke. He had to reach the shore. The strong current carried him downriver toward the dam. The roller gate was up. The water that flowed down toward it got sucked under the gate.

He was not going to make it. He was being swept along faster than he could swim toward the shore.

"Bill!" he heard Robin call. "Grab on!" She held out a long dead branch. He shot out a hand as he went by her. His hand caught the branch and somehow he managed to hold on. The current still pulled him downstream, but he swung in an arc as he held onto the branch. He was on his back as he collided with the rocks. His bottom would be bruised, but he was no longer in danger of going through the roller gate. He scooted his sore wet butt up onto the rocks, lay back, and panted. Robin plopped down next to him and also panted. They watched the raft collide with the nearest roller gate, hung there for a few seconds, and then got sucked under.

"That was so close," he said.

"You would have got sucked right under just like our raft," Robin said. "You'd be dead right now."

He nodded, staring at the rocks under his feet. "Yeah!"

She punched him hard in the shoulder. "Don't you dare leave me alone." She stared at him as he rubbed his shoulder, and then she laid back against the boulders. "Don't you dare leave me."

He stared up at the sky. The sun had just set, and the sky was bright pink at the top of the hills. They were screwed. He swore every four-letter word he knew at the top of his lungs. He grabbed a rock and hurled it at the waves in a scornful attempt to extract revenge upon the river. The river just flowed uncaring.

Robin put her hand on his shoulder. She leaned toward him and then laid her head on his shoulder next to her hand. He heard her sniffle. "What do we do?" she asked.

He wiped away a tear from her face with a finger. He didn't know what to say. She was always the strong one. "Charlie and Rose lost their craft to a storm too."

"Did they make it."

"Yeah. Toward the end, they were captured by the Germans and were about to be hung as spies. But at the last moment, they were saved by their old boat. The German boat on which they were being held ran into the hull of the *African Queen*. Its bomb sunk the German boat, and they swam away to safety."

She laughed a little laugh. "Don't think our raft's going to save us. We didn't even name her. The raft, I mean."

"Yeah. She was a good raft, the *Dinosaur World Queen*." He sat up. "We just got cocky trying to cross in this weather."

Robin laughed. "Stupid name for a raft."

"Is *Doomed Raft* better?"

She smiled. "Who gets to tell DeJuan what happened to the raft he built?" She shivered. "I'm freezing."

Bill also shivered in his wet clothes. They had to get warm or they would die of hypothermia. "Come." He lifted them both to their feet. "We're still alive and we're gonna stay that way. We're just going to have to save each other."

He grabbed the stick she used to rescue him. Their spears were gone, so the stick was their only weapon. They were both soaking wet, and the cold wind blew in their faces. Bill shook as he said, "Let's get up on top of the dam. The lock is on the other end. There is a control building there. Maybe we can get inside it and spend the night. Maybe, even find a way to warm up. We'll figure out what to do next in the morning."

"How are we ever going to make it?" she asked.

"One step at a time." He looked at her wet motley hair as it whipped in the wind. "But together." With arms around each other, they climbed to the top of the dam.

"Shit! Bad enough we lost the raft, we lost the damn radio too," Robin said. "How are we going to get a message back to everybody at the mall?"

"Try to see the bright side."

"There's a bright side to this?"

Bill chuckled. "At least we don't have to tell DeJuan what we did to his raft."

Chapter 27 - Robin

F irst things first," Bill said. "Let's just get through the night."

They climbed up the bank of limestone rocks to the berm on top. Once they had climbed, they saw the berm cut across the upper tip of a small island, covered with trees and tall grass. To their left the spillway structure stretched across the channel on that side of the island. A set of steel tracks ran down the middle of the berm from the spillway up to the dam. A ramp carried the tracks to the top of the dam.

They climbed the ramp up to the dam structure and walked across. About a quarter of the way across, a large red crane sat on the rails and blocked their path. Not enough room to get around it, but there were steps up onto the crane's platform and around and down the other side. Robin glanced at the control tower. It stood next to the locks by the far shore, another 700 feet across the dam from them. As they hiked, daylight quickly disappeared, and stars appeared overhead.

Robin shivered in the breeze as they approached the control tower. Bill had to be just as cold. "Our luck this place will be locked up tight," Robin said.

"It's all windows," Bill replied. "If we have to, we'll break one with a rock."

They found the door under the darkening sky and turned the handle—it wasn't locked. But inside the place was very dark despite all the windows. There wasn't even a moon to provide light.

"Hello?" Robin shouted. She didn't expect an answer and didn't get one. It felt spooky.

"Any drawers you can find, feel around inside for anything useful to us," Bill said.

Robin's hands trembled from the cold as she found a drawer in a desk by the entrance. She felt small boxes, loose paper clips, rubber bands and pens. Not helpful. Suddenly a bright beam of light shone in her face and blinded her.

"Sorry about that," Bill said. "Found a flashlight." He turned the light back to where he found it. "Hey, here's another one." He handed her the light.

She flicked it on. It wasn't as bright as Bill's. The batteries were probably old. The beam helped her to see what she searched though. They continued to look around and found newer batteries for Robin's flashlight. Then they found a cabinet with work uniforms in it. They both agreed to turn off the lights while they changed from their wet clothes into the uniforms. Robin finished quickly and turned her light on at Bill.

"Hey, I'm not done yet," he yelled.

"Sorry." She laughed. What she was really sorry about was she hadn't caught him earlier. He already had the pants on.

"Look what I found in the pocket," Bill said. His light was back on and illuminated a book of matches. "By the smell of this uniform, I'd say it belonged to a smoker."

Robin shivered. "Damn, it's cold in here. Think we could get a fire started with those?"

"If we can find something to burn."

They searched for a short time longer, but they couldn't find anything unless they were going to burn the furniture. They considered that, but, after a short discussion, they hiked back in the dark over the dam to the island to where they had come ashore instead.

There was plenty of deadfall there. Under the light of their flashlights, they quickly filled trash cans they brought with them from the control tower with kindling and firewood from the island. Bill carried the filled cans and Robin dragged along an additional large dead branch back to the dam.

They headed back and were near the top of the ramp when a scraping sound on the gravel came from behind them. Robin whipped her light back along the track. Two large silvery eyes reflected the light.

"Run!" she yelled.

Bill dropped the cans as she let go of the branch, and they both ran as fast as they could. The flashlights lit the path ahead. The footsteps of the giant pounded the track behind them. She couldn't tell from the quick glance what was after them, but it was big.

They had to get over the crane. Maybe that would stop the monster, she hoped. It was their only chance.

Bill reached the steps of the crane first and jumped up onto its platform without touching the steps. He disappeared around the side as she jumped to repeat his act. Her foot caught the edge of the top step. She sprawled out on the platform and banged her back into the base of the crane's cab.

Her flashlight pointed back at the creature. It was a huge sailback, and its long skinny snout full of long sharp teeth loomed closer.

Then her arm was being jerked. Bill dragged her around the platform. She got back to her feet and scooted around to the far side of the cab just as the toothy snout of the carnivore came around the corner. They were just out of its reach. Jumping off the other side of the platform, they turned to run again.

Robin considered her options. If the monster got past the crane, they would not be able to outrun it. She stopped. Could they jump into the river? She thought about it as Bill ran across the dam. No, the river would be as sure to kill them as the sailback. Even if they managed to not drown because of the undercurrents, they would have a long way to swim in strong currents before making it to shore. And if they somehow miraculously made it to the shore, they would probably succumb to hypothermia.

Bill suddenly stopped running.

"Run, you fool," she yelled. If the monster got around, she planned on sacrificing herself. That might give Bill just enough time to reach the control room and save himself. But the fool ran back to her.

Loud banging noises came from behind her. She turned her light back toward the crane. The monster had one leg on the platform and the other was stretched up on top of hood of the crane. It crawled over the crane. It seemed hopeless. There was nothing they could do to stop the beast.

Its third leg sprung up onto the hood. Then its second leg stepped off the hood. The first leg came off the platform and stepped onto the deck of the dam.

The third leg came down off the cab, but it caught in the cable snaked up through the crane. The sailback lost its balance and tottered and then fell against the railing on the upriver side of the dam. The railing buckled under the monster's weight and the beast fell on the crushed railing. Its legs scratched for a hold on the dam deck as it attempted to right itself. Its third leg popped free from the cable that held it.

But then the railing tore away from the dam. The dinosaur tumbled over the edge and plunged into the river. There was an enormous splash and a high-pitched shriek was audible even over the deafening roar of the water rushing through the dam's gates. Then there was only the roar of the gates.

Robin turned toward Bill and put her hands on her hips. "Why the heck didn't you run? I tried to buy you some time."

"We're in this together. If we die, we die together. I'm not going on without you."

She wanted to pound on him again, but instead put her arms around him and held him tight for a minute.

With the sailback gone, they turned around and retrieved their firewood before returning to the control tower. A fire was started on the concrete just outside the entrance door to the tower. They pulled out a couple of office chairs from around the desks and sat next to each other in front of the fire.

The warmth of the fire felt good on Robin's face, and she could feel its warmth through the front of the uniform she wore. Her bare feet had been covered with a spare shirt they found in the cabin. She freed her toes, wiggled them, and let them bask in the fire's warmth. Robin stared at their shoes and socks as they dried near the flames. She put her head down on Bill's shoulder. She thought about his unwillingness to let her sacrifice herself for him, and she soon fell asleep.

She woke and realized the pink sun had just peaked over the ridge to the east. She watched as Bill tossed the last two sticks onto the fire.

"Get any sleep at all?" she asked.

"A few winks." He yawned.

She yawned too and stretched. There were cricks in her back and neck from having slept in the chair. "Don't suppose there's breakfast."

252 : MJ Konkel

Bill laughed. "Breakfast? We don't even have drinking water. We lost our cooking pan. We lost everything." He looked around. "What do we do from here?"

"We saw a house last night and this dam structure is here," said Robin. "Brown's Station must be close. We hike downriver."

"All right. Let's look inside first and see if there's anything we can use for protection."

Robin stared at Bill's pants as he got up. "Are those pants or capris?"

Bill laughed. "I guess there was no one here my size."

A half-hour later they crossed the gate across the locks. They were thankful the gates, with their four-foot-wide walkways, were closed. They walked across instead of having to swim. From there, they followed a road up to a highway which ran parallel to the hills and river.

The pair hiked south using as walking sticks a pair of broomstick handles they had found. The hollow metal tubes tinked softly on the road's blacktop with each set of steps. They had attached a screwdriver to one end of each, using an entire roll of duct tape since the butts of the screwdrivers didn't fit into the broomsticks. That made for a big ball of tape on each broomstick with the sharp screwdriver sticking out of it, pointing toward the sky as they hiked.

After an hour they stopped for a rest. They were excited after Bill pointed to the south. A church steeple stuck out above the treetops. It had to be Brown's Station. Maybe they would make it after all.

But then a twig snapped, and Robin whipped her head around. A raptorsaur strutted through the woods about fifty feet away from them. "Bill!"

"I see it. There's another farther up the road too." Bill nodded in its direction.

Damn! There were at least two of them. Robin quickly scanned around as she got to her feet but didn't see a third. She spotted a concrete culvert though which went under the road less than ten yards away from them.

She pointed at it for Bill. "In there!"

They slowly stepped backwards toward it and held their weapons pointed at the closest raptor. It strutted up and cautiously inched closer; its head bobbed as it approached.

Robin dove into the culvert, and Bill followed right behind her. It was big enough for them to get in on their hands and knees. Robin spun around on her knees as her head brushed the top of the culvert, and Bill did the same next to her. They both pointed their modified broomstick weapons toward the opening. Robin glanced over her shoulder at the other end of the culvert. It had a thick metal grate over it to catch debris. The raptors could only get at them from the side they had come in.

A head appeared in front, and two beady eyes stared in at them. Robin thrust her weapon at the head and Bill did the same a moment later. Each caught a cheek with a screwdriver. The raptor pulled away with a loud squawking sound. That one would have matching scars. Robin and Bill held out their weapons ready for another raptor to appear.

"Think the other one'll try to get at us?" Robin asked.

"I'm ready if it does." Bill held his weapon pointed toward the opening.

A blast came from somewhere outside.

"That sounded like a gun," Bill said.

"Yeah," Robin inched forward and poked her head out of the opening. An animal stared from a short distance back at her.

But she relaxed. It was only a dog. "Hello," she called out. The dog stopped and gave a bark as it wagged its tail in a friendly greeting. Then it turned its gaze up onto the road.

"Hello, down there." The freckled face of a tall young woman with long curly brown hair appeared over the edge of the road. As she cradled a shotgun in her arms, she set a foot up on something. "There're over here," she called back up the road. "You're not from around here, are you?" It was a statement really, rather than a question.

Robin stood and saw the woman's foot rested on a dead raptor.

"How did you find us?" Robin asked as Bill squeezed out of the culvert behind her.

"We were coming up to the spillway to do some fishing. The spillway traps the spawning sturgeon there. That's when we saw smoke coming from over by the dam. Didn't know anybody was there, so we went to check it out. From there, Nova tracked you down." The woman patted the retriever on the side. "I'm Anne Loinka, and my friend here is Johnny Faberley. I take it you're not here to rescue us."

Robin laughed before she told them their long story and listened to theirs.

Chapter 28 – Mall

It was almost five o'clock. Almost everyone, including An Dung, crowded around the shortwave receiver on the seventh and topmost level of the East Parking Ramp. There had been no messages the past two evenings, which had started a lot of speculation about what might have happened to Robin and Bill.

Many people had died already because of the animals, so people were prepared to believe the worst. Robin and Bill could have been killed or badly wounded by a dinosaur or alligator. Or something they haven't even come across yet. They could have capsized and drowned. Or not drowned but lost the radio. The old radio could have simply stopped working for a number of reasons. After all, it was so old it still used vacuum tubes. Or maybe they were out of range. Everyone hoped some incident merely caused them to not be able to send a message at the designated times, and they would send a message this time.

As they all listened, they only heard steady static. Somebody chattered in the back of the crowd. Joel hushed them to silence. DeJuan waited with a notepad ready to scribble down the dots and dashes of the message if there were any.

Then they heard the static interrupted and then a message, but it was not in Morse code. Everyone was shocked to hear Bill's voice, loud and clear.

He explained they made it to a place called Ridgeback Island and the folks there had a thriving community in a safe location.

There was an explosion of cheers and Joel had to hush the crowd to be able to hear the rest of the message. They learned how they had gotten transported to this world and how there was a rescue in progress. Bill also told them about their adventures down the river and how they capsized. He told them they were being mighty quiet and hoped they were listening.

Everyone laughed.

Bill told them that the people at Ridgeback had worked to get a fleet of three pontoon boats and several smaller boats around the dam earlier in the day. They would be leaving in the morning and expected to get up to the mall by sundown the next day to bring them all down to their community where they had a safe location and a thriving little community.

From there, they would be going home! They could say good-bye to the dinosaurs.

Cheers erupted at the mall.

Epilogue

Everyone still alive at the mall safely made it down to Ridgeback Island and joined the community there. When everyone learned the mall people were poofed mere hours after the Professor had left to go back to their home world, they were encouraged. That meant the professor and the few others from Ridgeback must have made it home. They faithfully waited for the expected rescue to imminently arrive. Weeks passed, months passed, and then years, and still no rescue.

Some people quickly, some slowly, came to conclude the expected rescue was never going to happen, and they set about making a home out of their new world.

~ The End ~

From the Author

I hope you enjoyed reading this book. If you would be so kind as to leave a review, it would be much appreciated. Even if it is something short like "best dinosaur book ever" or "stunk like bronto gas." Hopefully, not the latter. You can leave it on Amazon and/or on Goodreads.

If you enjoyed this book, great! If you are interested in hearing about my upcoming novels, what it is like to be an author, or would love to know when deals are available and other cool stuff, join my newsletter. Note that your email address will only be used by me to send you my newsletter. Nothing else. You will find the link to my newsletter sign-up on my website at

http://www.mjkonkel.com

If you have comments about the book you would like to send directly to me, I would be delighted to receive them. You can find me on Goodreads or send them to

michael@mjkonkel.com.

Thank you and ROCKet ON!

****

For your enjoyment, here is a sneak preview of the first book in M.J. Konkel's Dinosaur Country Series. Kat is the daughter of Anne Loinka and Johnny Faberly, characters only appearing near the end of this book but who were central in No Road Out.

No Mercy in Dinosaur Country
by M.J. Konkel

Chapter 1

"George!" Kat called out.

She sighed as she sat back, clearly ignored. Her eyes panned around, taking in the alien-like world. Even though still technically a version of Earth, it was far different from the one on which she had been born. And that one was even more different than the one on which her parents grew up. At the moment she missed the world she called home.

She desperately needed time to unwind—away from the rest of the crew and the bickering which had become infectious as of late. Being on the fly hopping from world to world had worn her down. Her eyes closed for just a moment as she took in a deep breath. The rest of the crew were just as tired, but they weren't to blame any more than herself. They all badly needed a break and no more excitement for a while.

"George!" she called out again. Still ignored.

Off on the northern horizon stood tall mountains of ice. Not where she and her crew were headed, but the glaciers were responsible for the way the land had been sculpted and the way the animals had developed on this world. A reminder there are always forces more powerful than humans in shaping the universe. As alien as this world seemed, it still had a certain appeal to her. It had spots one could sit and hear nothing but the whispering wind. There was the abundance of wildlife with a few truly spectacular animals, and she never tired of watching them. Only of having to talk about them.

Flinging her long auburn pigtails in an arc around her head, Kat turned until her eyes locked onto George. She had been ignored long enough. "For cripes sake, George. Stop fricking ignoring me. It was you who insisted on getting this last shoot in. So, are we doing this or what? If you want to call it off, just let us know, and I'll be fine with it. I'm sure the same for the guys." She heard the edge to her tone when she spoke but felt she lacked control over it. She sighed a second time. It was weariness, really. Nothing a long vacation couldn't fix.

Her producer, George DeMooney, glanced in her direction and harrumphed. George also did the directing and half the filming. "I heard ya the first time. And the second. Just keep your Glocks in their holsters." He scratched the top of his shiny forehead, rubbed his hand over what little remained in the back, and then returned back to his fiddling.

Kat rolled her eyes. She had only one Glock on her, a 19C Gen6, but it was not worth the effort to correct him with a retort over that.

"And don't fricking shoot off my butt with them just 'cause I'm the one holding us back this particular morning. It's not like you're always on time." He pointed down at the gadget in front of him. "Been fricking struggling to get this new camera to work. For the show, you know. It'll make it better."

Kat sighed. He was right about her not always being on time, but right now he was being the problem. "You've been fiddling with that all week. Maybe it's time to just give it up."

"Yeah, no tech support out here, you know. But I finally figured out what I've been doing wrong."

"Oh, for all the heavens' sake, can't you just use one of your old ones? This is our last shoot of the season, is it not?" Kat didn't like how every little thing irritated her.

"Camera tech's my area," George snapped back. "It's not like I tell you—"

"Tell me what?" Kat glared at him.

"Never mind." George shook his head, trying to brush it aside.

Kat couldn't quite let go just yet. "How to stand? How to point? You tell me how to do everything except—"

"I'm your director." George cut her off before she could finish the crude remark that dangled on the tip of her tongue. He broke eye contact with her and fiddled with his camera again and then mumbled, "I just want this to be a good episode."

Yes, Kat had to admit he was always trying to make the episodes better. The consummate perfectionist. But she wondered how much his persistence with the gadget was due to his stubbornness to get something out of it before the end of the trip since he had paid a bundle to have it meet up with them in time after being backordered. "We've been shooting darn footage for six long days. There's got to be enough to piece together a decent episode."

"Yeah, well, we could. But it just feels to me to be missing something that could make it ... um ... special. Hoping this camera can get us that special something."

"The animals on this world aren't special enough?"

"There." He ignored her question as he popped a panel back in place. "I got it working now, so don't get your ..." George cut himself off and mumbled something unintelligible to himself instead. He glanced down at his watch and then turned back to Kat. "Let's get this last footage done, and then we can all get the hell out of here. Shuttle's set to arrive in just over five hours."

Kat's eye caught Jose and Ricky heading over. Jose was throwing up a hand and yelling something at Ricky, and Ricky was not taking any of it. Kat definitely did not have a monopoly on crankiness. The problem was they had been shooting episodes week after week for nearly six months, and they all sorely needed a break. Time away from each other.

Kat turned back to George. "What's so darn special about this camera anyway?"

George chuckled as he leaned over into a carboard box and pulled out a huge case. Inside was what looked like a miniature blimp, complete with tiny stubby wings and propellers attached. "Camera mounts to this. It's the latest in drones. Filled with helium to give buoyancy. Not just quiet, but totally silent. The only downside is it can't be used if winds are too high." He grinned from ear to ear.

Getting the camera working had given George joy, and that somehow irritated Kat. "Or if there is a football game nearby."

"Very funny." George faked a chuckle. "Nobody's tossing my camera. This baby's mine."

Kat shook her head as she rose. It was not that she couldn't see the value in the new camera drone; it was just that she wanted to be done with the shoot. Get back to civilization and sleep on a soft mattress in a real bed instead of on a hard cot in a tent.

George rose from the table where he had been sitting, signaling to everyone he was finally ready.

"Let's get on with it then." Kat peered toward the west. They would have to hike out to where they had last seen the animals, shoot their footage, and still get back in time. The last thing she wanted was to be late getting back. Hopefully, the animals were still in the vicinity of where they had been last spotted, or the whole morning was going to be a big waste.

"Right. But you better spit out whatever sour apple you bit into before we start shooting. I need Katgirl, not Tartgirl in front of the camera when we start shooting." George squinted at her a moment longer before turning his head. "Jose, grab your gear. Ricky, you carry this case for me. We're heading out."

Kat crossed her arms and frowned. However, she knew he was right. She needed to cheer up before the filming started. Or at least act like she had once the cameras were rolling.

"Nothing but a fricking mule," Ricky mumbled as he reached for the case.

George ignored the comment and turned toward the tall older man who had just exited the closest tent. "Doctor Toulouse, you're welcome to join us."

The doctor was the scientist kind of doctor. He called himself a mammalogist while some of the others on his small team called themselves ethologists. They were here on the world to study the animals just because that's what scientists do. They study things.

"I'd really love to, but I've got samples I need to make sure are properly packed for the shipment back to Prime." Dr. Toulouse stroked his bushy red beard with two fingers. "Just make sure you're back in time before the shuttle leaves. They stick to their schedules and won't be back again for another week." Kat could see Toulouse had tired of their irritability too and didn't want any part of it. She didn't blame him.

"We'll be back in plenty of time. Let's move out," George called as he turned and followed Kat.

Toulouse was the reason Kat and her team had been able to come to the world. Worlds like the one they were on had some of the most interesting wildlife in the multiverse but could only be accessed via the science teams' supply shuttles. Luckily, Toulouse was a big fan of their show and thrilled when George asked if he could bring his small film crew. Most scientists he had contacted simply said no. They didn't want a video team messing up their pristine research environments, as if George and Kat's presence were really going to make a difference. But after a week of the filming crew being around, even Toulouse had apparently gotten his fill of them.

Kat led the way as they marched across the tundra, colored red and yellow by the moss and small bushes that covered the rocky terrain. A warm dry breeze blew from the south, probably not strong enough to prevent George from trying out his new toy. In the distance to the north stood what appeared to be mountains but actually were glaciers, extending far to the south on the continent; the same ones Kat had stared at earlier.

This was an alternate Earth, $Earth_{1912}$ to be precise. The 1911th alternate Earth to be catalogued back at $Earth_1$, also called Earth Prime or simply Prime. Kat was reminded of an Earth similar to $Earth_{1912}$ which she had been on half a dozen years prior when the ship she had been on was lost. That version of Earth also had a North America locked in the grips of an ice age.

She topped a knoll and stopped, waiting for the others to catch up. A wide valley spread out below. Unlike the rocky terrain they had just hiked across, the valley was bright green with fast-growing grass. A shallow milky river wound through the center of the valley which stretched to the left as far as the eye could see. To the right, it wound around a bend and continued beyond their sight up toward the glacier.

Down in the valley a few hundred yards away, six magnificent giants grazed on the verdant grass of the wet valley. Woolly mammoths.

Kat glanced back at the others. George already tugged on his new drone with its camera from the case Ricky had carried. She wondered, as she watched the small skinny kid next to George push his wire-rimmed glasses back up higher on his nose, whether he would be back after their much-needed break. The kid, barely out of high school, seemed homesick most of the time. But mostly, Kat had sensed George was a little disappointed in him. Off to the left of George, Jose carried a second camera in his big muscular arms and already had it pointed at the giants.

George was right. She needed something to put herself into a better mood. She thought back to when they were on Earth$_{98}$, a mostly water world with a few archipelagos. She had placed an eye patch with its elastic strap over one of the 3D camera's two lenses when George had turned his attention elsewhere. Then she kept pointing out across the surf and saying things like "Aargh! Thar she blows," and "Aargh! Load the monkey," until he finally figured out why his camera had suddenly stopped working right. Afterward he laughed along with her and the rest of the crew. She smiled at the memory and reminded herself he really was a good man, just a little obsessed at times.

She turned her attention back to the mammoths and assessed where to do the shoot. George would also be looking, but he would be using only his artistic eye. She would have the final say on where she stood, taking into consideration her own safety. After all, when it would be her butt closest to the fire, she had the right to say what was too hot. An outcrop of rocks a little to the right of the animals caught her eye. The rocks weren't a big enough barrier to really stop an irate animal if it decided to charge, but the rocks should at least slow it down. Besides, six days of being around the animals had given her a sense of their temperament which was generally pretty gentle. She pointed the spot out to George, and he squinted at it for several seconds and then nodded his approval. She eased down to the spot, not wanting to spook the animals, and knowing George needed time to get his camera in an optimal position.

Once she reached the rocks, she pulled out a pad and used its camera to check her appearance. She made a minor adjustment to her hair in front and brushed one of her pigtails back. She had wanted to cut her hair short, but George insisted she keep the tails. They had become a hallmark of her video persona. The young woman known as Katgirl, the new outdoor video star of *The Wild Multiverse*.

"How do I look? As good as Emily Von Strife?" The actress. Kat smiled at George as she rolled up her pad and stuck it into her hip pocket.

"Better." George stared at his pad as Kat looked straight at his camera.

"Eat your heart out, Emily," she muttered as she turned, smiled, and gave a profile, followed by a spin on her heals to give the opposite cheek. She knew he had told a lie—no woman was in Von Strife's league. But it still felt good to hear it.

He saw everything through his screens. He flashed a thumb skyward. "Good. Go with it, anytime you're ready." He kept the cameras recording much of the time since modern file storage capacity was so high. He and a team back on Earth Prime would later splice together what was best for the program. It also gave them lots of extra stuff to use for later behind-the-scenes episodes.

"It's our last day here on Earth nineteen twelve, and I must admit I'm going to miss this world when we leave in a few hours." She blinked at the camera Jose held and then pivoted her head toward the mammoths. "I am especially going to miss these animals behind me. Gentle peaceful giants. Like the broncos on my home world, there is something—"

"Stop, stop, stop." George lowered his pad controlling the drone camera and shook his head.

"—majestic." Kat squinted at George. "What?"

"You said broncos instead of brontos."

"I did not, did I? That makes no damn sense. Why would I—"

"You need to see the fricking recording yourself?" George lowered his gaze to his pad without waiting for a reply. "Just take it again from 'Like the brontos' and continue from there. We'll splice it later."

Kat took a breath in and turned her head back toward the mammoths. "Like the brontos on my home … Whoa! What the frick's going on?"

The closest mammoth had turned toward them and stomped a few steps forward. It raised its big, curved tusks outward and then suddenly let out a loud trumpeting sound much like that of an angry elephant. Clearly a warning. The other adult mammoths quickly turned and faced Kat and the crew as well. All seemed riled. Only the lone juvenile remained to the rear of the herd.

Startled, Kat stepped backward. The crew had been filming the mammoths for nearly a week without any sign of aggression from them. She had even been much closer to the animals on one of the earlier sessions. Doctor Toulouse, who had been around the creatures far longer than they had themselves, had assured them mammoths never seemed bothered by any of the researchers being in their vicinity. Why then were these animals suddenly behaving like this?

"It's that damn thing." Kat pointed at the new camera drone hovering near the animals.

"They're looking our way—not at the fricking camera," George said.

He was right. Kat stared at the mammoths, but they seemed to stare back right through her. Past her. She suddenly had the feeling of being watched and not by them. She spun her head around.

A large cat eyed them from atop a boulder some fifty yards away. It had a gray coat which blended into the bare rocks around it. What stood out, though, were the two huge canines clearly visible even from the distance. The doctor had warned about the saber-toothed cats being around, but Kat and George had not seen one in their week of filming. Now a brute easily topping 400 pounds stared at them through large dark eyes.

"Guys, behind us. Back up out of here," Kat said. "Whatever you do, though, don't turn and run." She reached down and pulled the Glock out of the holster on her thigh. The pistol held fifteen 9-mm jacketed hollow-point rounds in its magazine, plus one in the chamber. She hoped she didn't need to use more than a few of the rounds, though, and then only to scare the cat off.

"What do we do if it attacks us?" Jose's voice quivered.

"Stay behind me." Kat's eyes remained glued squarely on the cat in front of her. "If I have to, I'll put him down, but I really hope it doesn't come to that. Nobody be stupid about this and turn tail. He'll see you as prey and run you down, and you can bet your sweet ass he's faster than you. Just keep walking backward and keep an eye out for others coming from the side. And for cripes sake, don't trip and fall."

"What others?" Jose's voice rose. "Where?"

272 : MJ Konkel

"Just watch for others." Kat stepped backward quickly. Each step carefully placed so her footing remained solid.

Behind her, someone tripped and fell. Kat didn't have to glance back to know it was Ricky. Rocks scraped against each other as he scrambled back to his feet.

The cat stretched out its paws, dropped off the rock, and disappeared. Only to reappear as it hopped onto the top of a boulder a bit closer. It dropped off the second boulder and trotted toward them, moving faster than them. The gap between them and the cat quickly shrank.

Kat stopped and held her ground. "Hey, buddy! That's close enough." She squeezed the trigger and fired off a single round. Rock splinters flew up in front of the cat. It sprang back a step, displaying fast reflexes, and dropped into a crouch. Its nostrils flared wide.

"There are two ... two more above us," Ricky said. "We're surrounded. Whatta we do?"

Kat sneaked a quick glance at the other two cats. Still more than fifty yards away, they trotted along the valley's rim.

The cat in front of her rose slowly out of its crouch as the other cats drew closer. Kat squeezed off another round and rocks flew up again in front of the first cat.

It did not jump back this time. Its jaws opened wide, and a guttural snarl came from the cat, telling Kat it was not afraid of her. She didn't buy it though. The cat was wary of them. Otherwise, it would have already pounced. The other two cats were now almost as close as the first cat, and Kat swung her pistol at them before pointing it back toward the first cat.

She took careful aim and squeezed off a third round. The pointed tip of the cat's right ear suddenly disappeared in less than an eyeblink. Only a ragged red edge remained. The cat sprang five feet straight up into the air, screeching. It legs barely seem to touch back to the ground before it spun and sprang back away. Rocks and dust were kicked up as the cat leaped over the rocks above them.

Kat swung to her right, pointing her pistol toward where she had last spotted the other cats. One of the cats was there above them for just a moment, but then it too disappeared. The last one leaped to the rocks above and to the right of the other cats, and then it too was gone.

Kat had been right in her intuition. The first cat to appear was the alpha of the pack, and when it decided the humans were not easy prey, the others were not about to attack with their leader retreating.

She lowered her pistol but did not holster it. "Let's get back before that shuttle arrives."

"Hope there's time to change my pants." Jose glanced at Kat. "Holy buckets, that was scary."

"Are they, uh, really gone?" Ricky continued to stare at the spot where the cats had perched above them.

"Most likely," Kat said. "But keep sharp anyway. George, tell me you got that."

"Well, there was the difficulty of walking backwards and not tripping over the rocks," George said. "I have enough trouble just walking forwards."

"George?"

"And the fact that those lions were about to eat us. They saw us as big fat juicy steaks."

"George!"

"Yeah, of course, I got that. When have you ever known me to stop filming just because I thought we were about to die? Those are the scenes that are going to make a legend out of you. Not to mention drive up our ratings."

Kat rolled her eyes. "You're one of a kind. But you already know that, don't you, you son of a bitch?"

George laughed. "Yeah, well, right back atch ya. Lucky for me 'cause you're why I'm still here alive."

Kat cocked her head toward George. "I guess I was a little cranky earlier."

"A little?"

Kat laughed. "Hey, I said sorry."

"Actually, you didn't. Not yet anyway."

Kat holstered her pistol, not intending to say those two words. "Come on, I'll buy you a beer when we get back to Prime."

"Make that two beers, and you're forgiven."

Kat glanced at Jose and Ricky. Their eyes were still wide as if they had just spotted the grim reaper. Kat thought about it for a moment. The cat's canines were shaped a lot like the business end of a scythe.

She turned and headed back toward the base camp. Some time off back on her home world had to be less exciting, right? All it had was dinosaurs.

******

Continued in

Dinosaur Country Book 1: No Mercy in Dinosaur Country

About the Author

M. J. Konkel was born and raised in rural western Wisconsin. He had a brief military stint in the U.S Army and then went to school in Minnesota where he earned a B.S. and Ph.D. in chemistry. After living in New Jersey for a while, he is back in western Wisconsin with his wife, two kids, and assortment of animals.

You can contact him at michael@mjkonkel.com

Books by M.J. Konkel available from Amazon
Kindle as e-books, paperback, or hardback:

The Displaced Series
     Book 1: No Road Out
     Book 2: Roar of the Rex
     Book 3: Between Time and Space
Dinosaur Country Series
     Book 1: No Mercy in Dinosaur Country
     Book 2: Predators and Prey
     Book 3: The Definition of a Monster
Dangerous First Step
Boots of Oppression

Made in the USA
Monee, IL
26 October 2023

45225676R00163